Triple-Threat Patrol . . .

by
KENNETH GILBERT

illustrated by
ERNEST NORLING

THE JUNIOR LITERARY GUILD AND
HENRY HOLT AND COMPANY · NEW YORK

TO
GEORGE AND GLADYS
For their wise
counsel

Contents

Triple-Threat Patrol . . .

1 ... Danger Ahead

*G*ray seas, their crests foaming, leaped upward as though trying to reach a dark sky which seemed to hang but a few feet above the wind-whipped water. Puget Sound, the hundred-mile-long waterway which splits deeply into the northwest corner of Washington state, is never calm when a gale sweeps in from the North Pacific, and this summer storm was as violent as it had been sudden. Most small craft had already reached safe harbors.

But the two boys in the skiff were trapped. Crouched in their little fourteen-footer, gripping oars which they had unshipped when the outboard motor had gone dead after being drenched by waves, they seemed to be fighting a losing battle. Chuck Harmon, huskier of the two, was scared, which he would have gladly admitted if it would have done any good. Doc Peters, his lean, solemn features even more serious than usual, probably felt the same way. This was rugged!

Apparently their only hope lay in reaching one of the San Juan Islands, whose bulky shapes, indistinct in the spray-filled air, loomed just ahead. But to do that, the boys might have to beach the skiff in dangerous surf—which meant that they'd have to swim and risk being battered to death on the rocks.

Maybe Chuck could make it because of his strength, for he was sixteen and big for his age. In school he was a line-plunging fullback, while the slightly built yet wiry Doc—only a month his junior—was the quarterback who called the plays, depending on wits rather than brawn to beat down opposition. But it was going to take some fast thinking to get out of *this* situation!

Chuck blamed himself; he should have followed his friend's advice at the beginning. Now it was too late.

For the squall had struck quickly, with only a brief warning. The boys had seen the southwest sky blacken, then a frothy line of water, at first far astern but moving rapidly toward them. Doc had squinted at the sight and declared, "We'd better take shelter somewhere!"

But Chuck had been impatient to reach their destination—the big island of Orcas, not more than an hour's run distant. The skiff carried their sleeping bags and pup tent, cooking utensils; they had enough food to last for days. The motor was firing perfectly, and the storm might turn eastward without touching them.

"Just a capful of wind," Chuck had replied. "I'm

sure we can make Orcas. A good sailor," he added confidently, "doesn't skedaddle for port every time he sees a little squall coming.

"Anyway," and his freckled face creased in a grin, "if things should get really tough, Doc, you can always call Play Twenty-Two!"

It was a long-standing joke between them. In many a football game which had seemed lost because the team had become overtense, it had been Doc's coolness and confidence which had saved the situation. Calmly he'd tell them, "Guess we'll have to try Play Twenty-Two!" The team had understood that this was his way of telling them to settle down—for there *was* no Play Twenty-Two! He was merely telling them, "Let's get down to earth again!" They knew that he hadn't given up hope, that he had a new plan of attack. So they listened—and frequently went on to win.

Yet this time Chuck's sally had brought no answering smile to his friend's face. Doc was worried. Still, he made no protest as Chuck held the skiff on course until the squall struck them. The motor quit, and here they were. It was going to require more than Play Twenty-Two to get them out of their predicament!

Trying to keep calm as they each manned an oar and kept the skiff headed downwind and away from those menacing whitecaps, they couldn't escape panic entirely. Suddenly, one of the foaming crests lifted above them, then broke sharply, pouring water into the craft. They stopped rowing long enough to bail furiously before another wave came, for they were terrified at the prospect of letting the craft become so waterlogged that the weight of the motor would sink it. They hadn't bothered to take life jackets or even kapok seat cushions along; the precaution had seemed unnecessary. If the skiff went down, they were going to have to swim without any device to keep them afloat.

Chuck half turned and looked over one shoulder. Up ahead the nearest island was at least a quarter-mile distant; it looked large and heavily wooded. Yet its rugged shoreline was marked by a continuous line of white surf shooting high in the air. Death appeared certain if they tried to land there. Chuck leaned toward Doc and raised his voice above the eerie shrieking of the wind.

"Maybe," he yelled hopefully, "we can keep off-shore until we pass that island and find shelter in its lee!" To do that the skiff would have to quarter the onrushing waves for some distance, and it was doubt-ful if there was power enough in oars alone to ac-complish the fact; yet it was either that or risk the surf.

Doc shook his head negatively. Apparently he, too, had sized up the situation. His voice was strained with anxiety as he answered, "Can't be done! Got to land among those breakers, and take our chance!" Chuck nodded as though he knew all along that they had no real choice.

The skiff would be smashed on the rocks; only a strong swimmer could survive, and he'd have to be lucky, at that! Doc had never been an expert in water; his chances of survival were going to be slim. Yet if the prospect scared him, he kept his fear hidden. Chuck forgot his own fear, in admiration of his chum's courage; and suddenly he felt stronger and more confident.

He turned for another look ahead—and glimpsed something so unexpected that at first it scarcely seemed real. Then his hopes soared as though rescue was certain and only a matter of minutes away.

Not more than two hundred yards ahead, fighting her way slowly through the smoking seas, was a small tug, moving at a right angle across their course. Chuck yelled in delight at Doc, and pointed to the craft just as she rose on a wave. All they had to do now, it seemed, was to draw attention to their plight, and they would be saved; she was plainly seaworthy enough to ride out this storm.

For an instant they stared at her; then she vanished as the crest of a wave intervened. Chuck saw that she had a small tow of logs, for a cable was stretched tightly from her stern to a bobbing raft a hundred feet or more behind her. There was nobody in sight on the tug's deck, yet Chuck was certain that somebody in the wheelhouse had seen them, for the distance was short. But the tug kept on without slackening speed or making any other indication that the storm-tossed skiff had been spotted.

Impulsively, the boys seized their oars and began pulling with all their strength. Each seemed to understand what was in the other's mind—they would bring the skiff around to leeward of the tug, or even the tow of logs, which would lessen the force of the waves. With that shelter, meager though it might be, they could secure the skiff and be towed to harbor even if the squall did not blow itself out in the meantime.

Chuck thought, "It's our only chance! We've *got* to make it!" Yet he didn't waste breath telling Doc what was in his mind.

For a half-minute they pulled strongly; then, knowing that they must be close to the tug and its tow, they stopped and stood up, waving their arms and yelling. And this time they knew they had been seen!

The wheelhouse door opened and a man stepped outside, staring at them. A moment later he was joined by another man. The two appeared to be discussing the situation. Then the second man went back into the wheelhouse again.

"We've done it!" Chuck cried. "I'll bet they're going to stop until we can catch up! Got to use our oars again, Doc!"

But Doc did not obey. Instead, he told Chuck, "Hold it! Something queer is going on over there!" Chuck looked at the tug again, now barely a hundred yards distant, and understood what Doc meant.

Chuck saw that the second man had reappeared, and this time he was carrying a rifle! The man lifted the gun, and instinctively both boys dropped low in the skiff. Because the howling wind carried most of the sound away from them they scarcely heard the

6

report of the gun, yet they saw the top of a nearby wave ripped through by a bullet. They eyed each other in amazement and alarm.

Finally Doc exclaimed, "That wasn't meant in fun! But why?"

Chuck had no answer. Here was a mystery so perplexing that momentarily the boys forgot they were in danger from the storm. The men in the tug were plainly warning them to stay away. The men on the tug surely realized that the boys needed help, but apparently that help wasn't going to be given. Instead, the skiff and its occupants could sink, for all that the strangers cared.

No more gunshots came, although the boys crouched low and waited. When several minutes passed and they dared raise themselves, they could see that the tug and its tow had passed on. Both men had gone back into the wheelhouse, apparently satisfied that the warning had been understood.

Wind and waves drove the skiff onward, headed straight for the beach, which was now so close that the thunder of the surf could be heard distinctly. Chuck told himself, "Won't be long now. I'll stick with Doc, if I can; maybe we can help each other." Aloud he said, "Let's shuck our clothes while we have a chance!"

But Doc replied hopefully, "Maybe we won't have to. Look yonder! This might be Play Twenty-Two coming up!"

Surprised at Doc's words, Chuck turned and peered ahead. Then Doc's meaning became clear.

7

There was one spot where the white line of surf was broken! The blank spot was marked by jagged rocks on either side. "A cove!" Chuck cried. "There's quiet water inside!"

Doc grinned jubilantly. "Grab your oar!" he directed. "If we pull hard and keep headed right, we'll break through—for yardage!" Chuck grinned back at him. It was like a tough football game. Doc, the signal caller, the field general, had spotted weakness in the enemy's line. Another Play Twenty-Two!

"Got to go through fast!" Doc reasoned. "If we don't, there may be currents which will pull us into those rocks on either side. *Now!*" They timed their strokes together, pulling with all their strength. The skiff responded, shot to the top of a wave, then down the slope of the opposite side. The roar of the nearby breakers filled the air, but Chuck didn't pause to look; he was putting his faith in Doc's planning and coolheadedness.

Once more the skiff rose, and with the muffled thunder of breaking waters sounding like a giant waterfall about to overwhelm them, Chuck fought hard against panic. He stole a look at Doc, and saw the latter's face strained with awareness of danger. Then came a hair-raising moment when the leaping surf soused into the skiff as though to founder it— but the next instant the angry seas were behind, and the half-filled craft moved sluggishly in quieter water.

They stopped rowing, eying each other in amazement and wonder. They'd made it! That was the

thing which seemed almost incredible. Safe! In their relief they'd even forgotten the mysterious tug and the warning shot fired at them.

Yet terror was still so fresh in their memory that neither boy felt like saying anything at once. They sat there in silence, almost too awed by the nearness of their escape, to speak. Yet as the wash of waves pouring through the entrance to the cove kept their waterlogged craft moving ahead slowly, they looked around the place in growing curiosity.

Chuck saw that the cove was larger than he had first guessed it would be. It was an irregularly shaped bay some five to six hundred yards across at its widest point. The entrance was merely a fifty-foot opening between massive rocks that were still lashed by the storm-whipped sea outside. It had been a miracle that they had been able to get through the narrow entrance at all!

Also it seemed to be a miracle that Doc had spotted this nearly hidden break in the surf. Surely he had sharp eyes!

Anyway, they were safe, and after they had beached the skiff and emptied the water out of her, they could build a fire, dry out their camping outfit and set up the tent, and they would no longer have anything to worry about. They could stay here until the drenched motor was overhauled and put in working condition once more, and perhaps by then the storm would have passed so they could resume their cruise to Orcas. Chuck felt cheerful, deciding that this tiny cove was going to prove to be an interesting place.

Surrounding the little harbor was a thick stand of old-growth fir, massive trees that were undoubtedly prime timber. So far as he could see this forest hadn't been touched by a logger's ax or saw. From the cove back toward the center of the island the ground rose steeply in a lofty "hogback" or ridge which was also covered by dense timber. The island was wild, primitive, almost forbidding.

Around the shore of the cove was a wide stretch of gray sand, an ideal spot for them to make camp until ready to continue their trip. There seemed to be plenty of driftwood for a fire, and maybe a spring of fresh water could be found although this wouldn't be immediately important as the skiff carried a gallon can of water for drinking purposes. Chuck had decided that it would be fun having the cove to themselves—and just then saw a raft of logs moored at the far end of the little harbor.

Somebody else was using this cove! He remembered the strange tug and its tow of logs, also the warning gunshot. Maybe the crew of the tug had wanted to scare the boys away, so that the cove would not be discovered!

Doc also saw the logs. "Maybe," he suggested, "we won't be welcome here! But," he pointed out, "there's no place else to go until this storm is over. So we'll have to stay! Suit you?"

"Suits me!" Chuck agreed. They resumed rowing, and soon the skiff touched shore. The boys got out, glad to feel solid ground under their feet.

There were signs that somebody had been here

recently—boot tracks in the sand, a scum of fresh sawdust on the water between the rafted logs and the beach, and also a V-shaped mark on the shore where a skiff had been landed. Chuck pointed out a dozen or more round, wooden disks strewn along the beach. They seemed to be of uniform thickness, about four inches, and it was plain that they had been cut from the ends of saw logs, such as those which were rafted within boom-length. Each had come from a good-sized log some four feet in diameter. Both boys walked closer to the disks, studying them in curiosity.

On one side of each disk was a brand-mark, apparently made by a steel maul. The brand consisted of two letters joined, forming the monogram, Ⱨ. Chuck looked inquiringly at Doc.

"Doesn't make sense," Chuck remarked. "What good are those wooden disks?"

Doc didn't answer at once. He peered again at the brand-mark, then looked out at the boomed logs. "They're no good," he replied, "unless they could be used as evidence."

"Evidence?"

"My guess," Doc went on, "is that these disks came from the ends of logs which used to be moored out there with that raft. They were sawed off because somebody wanted to get rid of the brand, so he could rebrand each log for himself."

"Log pirates?" There was a note of excitement in Chuck's voice.

Doc nodded. "Couldn't be anything else. If I had to make a guess I'd say that the tow of logs which that tug had, came from this cove. They pulled out of here just ahead of the storm. When they saw us they might have thought that we knew what had happened, and were trying to stop them. That's why they warned us off with a gunshot."

Chuck regarded Doc admiringly. No wonder the latter was a good quarterback. He had imagination. But in this case it was pure reasoning, cold logic.

"Doc," Chuck declared, "I think you're a hundred per cent right. And these wooden disks are evidence that logs have been stolen so they could be rebranded. Anyway, the pirates—whoever they are—have gone, and we have the cove to ourselves until this storm blows over. We're lucky to have made it!"

Doc looked at the storm-lashed entrance to the cove and nodded agreement. "We'd better get our outfit ashore and make camp," he said practically. "Then we'll go to work on the motor. Maybe we won't be staying here any longer than we have to."

"Why not? This is a cozy spot. Might be fun to hang around for a day or so and explore that wooded ridge—find out what's on the other side of it."

Doc shook his head. "Somebody owns those logs," he pointed out, "and it's likely the same person who owned the logs that were stolen. He'll be discovering what has happened before long. Besides, those log pirates may return. We could find ourselves in the middle of a scrap!"

Chuck seemed unimpressed. "What of it? We had nothing to do with it. None of our business."

"Sometimes innocent bystanders can get hurt!" Doc remarked sagely.

But at least they had an immediate job to do—drying out their equipment, getting the motor to work once more, and making camp for the night. There was not more than an hour of daylight left, and the still-overcast sky showed no sign of breaking, although it seemed that the wind was lessening. By morning, however, the storm should be gone.

Once their outfit was ashore, they began making camp. Their pup tent was set up, and as a windbreak for the fire they stood several of the wooden disks on edge in a half-ring before the opening of the tent. Getting a fire going wasn't much trouble, for there was an abundance of driftwood which had been washed well up on the beach during high tides in the past. Soon the flames were crackling in the fast-thickening gloom, and they began sorting out pieces of equipment which had been drenched by the waves, and draping them over the faces of the disks. Luckily their food had been packed in watertight wrappings to guard against such an emergency as had occurred. They detached the motor from the skiff, cleaned and dried the twin spark plugs, and at the first test it began firing perfectly once more.

Darkness had settled over their little camp when they had finished eating. But their clothing and sleeping bags were dry, and it looked as though they were going to spend a cozy night, their ordeal in the storm only a thrilling memory.

Neither, however, felt the need of sleep at once, even though they had made an early start that day. The situation was vaguely suggestive of unknown adventure. Behind their little camp was a strange forest which seemed wildly primitive; before them was the small cove whose waters whispered mysteriously in the dying gale, while overhead a few stars peered from a ragged sky. Chuck looked across the fire at Doc, and was glad that he was not alone. He had heard that there were one hundred and seventy-eight of these islands in the San Juan group, many of them uninhabited. He knew the names of only a few; neither he nor Doc knew the name of *this* one!

Not that it mattered. They'd have their outfit stowed aboard the skiff once more and be on their way to Orcas soon after daylight came. He thought again about the tug, the warning rifle shot. If the men aboard the tug towing the raft were actually log pirates, then this cove was no place to loaf until trouble caught up. Doc was right on that score.

Chuck stared into the fire a few minutes later, then yawned. "Going to turn in," he announced. He shot a questioning glance at Doc, expecting to see his friend nod agreement.

Instead, he saw an odd expression on the other's face. Doc, eyes widened, was staring *past* him, into the darkness beyond the ring of firelight!

"What's up?" Chuck demanded. Without waiting for an answer, he started to twist around to see what had attracted Doc's attention.

But as he did so, Chuck heard a voice behind him, sharply commanding, "Sit still, if you don't want to get hurt!"

2 ... Challenge

But Chuck had no intention of obeying the order. There was danger behind him—he could read as much in the expression on Doc's face—and it wasn't Chuck's nature to submit meekly to a challenge. He dropped both hands to the ground, preparing to leap to his feet, but Doc's voice stopped him. "Easy!" Doc counseled. "No use for anybody to get excited." And Chuck realized that Doc was speaking to the stranger, whoever he was.

There was silence for a moment; then Doc went on quietly, "All right, Chuck. Stand up, if you want to. But take it easy!"

Chuck got to his feet warily, and Doc did the same. Then Chuck turned slowly—and almost choked in astonishment!

Two or three paces from him stood another boy— slender, wiry, and so tanned that at first Chuck thought he was a young Indian. But the startling thing was that in his right hand, gripped like a spear, was a long pike pole armed with a steel point some four inches in length. The newcomer said slowly, "Don't try any tricks!"

At this threat, Chuck felt his own hackles rise. Despite the fact that the stranger was armed with a wicked-looking weapon, and that obviously he wasn't bluffing, Chuck felt fighting resentment stirring inside him. Quickly he sized up the other. If it was a battle this newcomer wanted . . .

"Easy, Chuck!" came Doc's warning voice. "Like I said, there's no call for anybody to get excited!"

Chuck made no reply, but continued his study of the stranger. The latter looked lean and muscular; his shoulders were as broad as Chuck's, although in height he was at least an inch shorter. About sixteen, Chuck guessed. The strange boy's hands were remarkably big, as though he was accustomed to doing heavy work. He was dressed in typical logger fashion—a shapeless red hat jammed on his head, checked flannel shirt with sleeves rolled up over his thick forearms, brown dungarees cut off at the bottom just above boots with eight-inch tops. He looked able and confident, and in battle he'd probably be a rough-and-tough foe even without that menacing pike pole. But Chuck had been smashing his way through burly tackles and line-backers too long to worry about odds being against him.

At the same time his curiosity as to the meaning of this extraordinary situation was so great that it nearly offset his inclination to meet violence with violence, if necessary. Who was this strange boy? Why was he so threatening?

It was Doc's quick thinking and natural calmness which saved the day.

"Look," he told the stranger, "we don't know who you are or why you're here, but there's no reason to declare war on us. Put down that frog-sticker, and tell us what's on your mind. Maybe we can be friends!"

For a long instant the stranger continued to eye both boys suspiciously, nor did he change his stance, but stood there with pike pole lifted. Chuck himself, taking the cue from Doc, felt curiosity growing and anger dying away. Presently the boy in the red hat seemed to understand that warfare wasn't imminent.

He lowered the pike pole, although still keeping it in readiness, and asked, "Who are you? What are you doing here? Some of the Jarvis gang, caught here in the storm and left behind?"

"Jarvis gang?" Doc repeated. "We don't know what you're talking about. We pulled in here to escape being drowned. What's wrong with that?"

The other pointed to the row of wooden disks standing around the fire. "You didn't saw off those cookies? You didn't steal my logs?"

Doc wagged his head in bewilderment. " 'Cookies?' " he repeated. "So that's what you call 'em." He paused and added, "Look, chum, you're all mixed up. We didn't saw off those 'cookies,' we didn't steal any logs, and we never heard of the Jarvis gang. All we know—"

Suddenly he broke off, and the firelight revealed understanding in his face. "Just before we reached this cove," he went on, "we met a tug with a small raft of logs. We tried to reach it because we were pretty sure we were going to founder. But one of the men aboard the tug took a shot at us with a rifle, so we kept clear, and managed to reach this cove just in time. We still don't know why they warned us to keep away. Does that make any sense to you?"

The newcomer was silent, apparently weighing what Doc had told him. For a long moment he looked hard at Doc as though trying to make certain that the latter was telling the truth. Finally he asked, "A small tug with a black funnel and two red stripes around it?"

"I remember the black funnel and red stripes," Chuck declared.

The other nodded. "Jarvis' tug, of course," he declared. "You," he told Doc, "make it sound like the truth."

"It is the truth!"

The stranger let out a gusty sigh. "Reckon it happened that way," he remarked. "They knew I was on the other side of the island, so they came here, sawed off those cookies and rebranded my logs; then they pulled out ahead of the storm. Maybe when they saw your skiff, they figured I was aboard, so they fired a shot as a warning to keep clear of 'em."

He took a long breath and added, "I'm sorry! But at the beginning it looked as though I'd caught two of Lem Jarvis' gang with the goods." He stepped nearer the fire and held out his hand, first to Doc, then to Chuck. As Chuck returned the stranger's grip he felt like wincing a little because the muscular fingers tightened like a vise.

"I'm Tim Elliott," the boy announced. "Live on the other side of the island with Gramps—Hank Elliott." He pointed to the brand on one of the wooden disks, and grinned fleetingly. "H.E.," he added with a touch of pride. "Some folks call him 'High Explosive' Elliott."

Doc flexed his own fingers after Tim had shaken hands, and said fervently, "I can understand *that*—with you as his grandson!"

Tim laughed. "Gramps and I try to take care of ourselves," he said modestly. "We have to—on Skookum-Chuck Island!"

"That's the name of this place?" Doc asked interestedly. "I don't know many words in the Chinook jargon, but my guess is that Skookum-Chuck means 'strong water.' "

Tim nodded. "That's because of the tide-rips about it," he explained. He pointed to the entrance of the cove. "You were lucky to reach here when the currents were just right, or you'd have been wrecked on those rocks."

A moment later he added, "These strong currents are one of the things that make it hard for me to keep Lem Jarvis and his gang from stealing our logs. Jarvis has a tug with a lot of power; all I have is a skiff and a pair of oars. Usually he waits until I'm on the other side of the island; then he slips in here and helps himself to our timber. Before I can buck the currents in my skiff, and stop him, he's gone!"

"What about Gramps?" Chuck asked. The question was impulsive, prompted by curiosity alone, yet the instant it popped out of him, Chuck regretted it.

Tim straightened, his face sober. "Gramps," he replied, "was crippled in an accident here two years ago. He'll never walk again!"

"Sorry," Chuck apologized quickly. "I didn't think—"

But Tim smiled as he broke in, "It's all right. No harm. Gramps homesteaded Skookum-Chuck years ago because of its timber—nearly three hundred acres of old-growth fir. We've cut some of it; but we're only hand-loggers—what folks up here call a 'chin-whisker outfit.' Yet," and his voice had a touch of pride, "we've worked out a scheme to handle these big sticks without machinery!

"I was born here," he continued. "Gramps raised me after my parents drowned when I was a baby. A freighter ran down their boat in a fog. If they hadn't left me behind that day, I'd have gone with them!"

His smile became almost apologetic. "I talk a lot, don't I?" he asked. "Especially to strangers!"

But Chuck felt warm sympathy. "Strangers? Look, Tim, I feel as though we'd known each other for years!"

"Same here!" Doc declared earnestly.

Tim nodded gratefully. "You're the first fellows my own age that I've met outside of those I know at

22

school. Guess I've been lonesome. No," he added, "that's not right. I'll never be lonesome as long as I have Gramps. And Kamooks!"

"Kamooks?" Chuck asked.

Tim turned toward the darkness and made a clucking sound. Out of the gloom a big, wolfish-looking dog appeared and stood by Tim's left knee, regarding Chuck and Doc with a steady gaze. The dog probably weighed more than a hundred pounds; his coat was blackish gray, and there was a odd-looking ring of white about each eye. His sharp-pointed nose twitched as he sampled the scent of the newcomers, but other than that he gave no sign that their presence interested him in the slightest.

"A Malemute?" Chuck asked.

Tim nodded. "An old sourdough friend of Gramps' sent him down from Alaska when Kamooks was still a pup. He's grown up here on Skookum-Chuck. But he's smart," Tim added proudly. "When I thought you were log pirates, and came up to look you over, he stayed back there in the dark, waiting to give me help, if I needed it!"

The dog did not move, but continued to regard the boys gravely, with no expression in his eyes, which in the firelight shone yellowish green. "It's all right, Kamooks," Tim told him. "They're friends. You can say 'hello.'"

The dog appeared to understand. He stepped forward, sniffing Chuck and Doc in turn. At last his bushy tail, curled over his back, wagged slightly, and he moved back beside his master, as though satisfied.

23

Tim grinned. "He says you'll do. From now on he'll always remember you as friends."

Doc remarked, "I'd hate to have him for an enemy!"

"Kamooks can take care of himself," Tim replied. He looked at the others. "Now that I've told you my story, maybe you'd like to tell me yours," he pointed out.

Chuck nodded. "It won't take long. Doc and I worked all winter in our spare time in order to buy this boat and motor. We've planned this San Juan Islands trip for a year. Next year we graduate, so this may be our last chance to have a vacation together. We'll spend the summer camping on Orcas—fishing, swimming, loafing, and doing whatever else we like."

Tim said enviously, "Wish I had that much spare time! I'll spend the summer cutting logs. If I work hard, maybe I can afford to go back to school. I'm a senior at Burlington High, on the mainland. An old fellow named Peterson comes here from Anacortes, and takes care of Gramps while I'm away."

He eyed Chuck interestedly. "You said your name is Harmon," he went on. "I've heard *that* name before! Is your father in the lumbering business?"

"He's general manager of the Sound Logging Company," Chuck explained. "Doc's father is woods superintendent of the same firm." Unconsciously, pride had crept into his voice. Sound Logging Company—as everybody must know—was the biggest timber outfit in the Pacific Northwest.

Yet, of a sudden, coolness came into Tim's manner.

24

He stared at Chuck. Then, after a long moment of awkward silence, he reached down and patted the dog's head. "Come on, Kamooks," he said, "we'll be getting home."

Chuck was mystified. "Anything wrong?" he asked curiously.

Tim replied stiffly, "Not a thing!" He looked off into the darkness. Outside the cove the wind was still moaning, and the rhythmic cr-ash of breakers about the entrance persisted, yet the storm was losing strength. In the sheltered cove the night was nearly calm. "How long are you going to stay here?" Tim asked abruptly.

"Pulling out tomorrow," Chuck answered. "Not later than noon."

Tim nodded as though satisfied. "I'll tell Gramps," he said. He was turning away when Doc stopped him with a gesture.

"Tim," Doc urged, "what's bothering you? If we're unwelcome here, we'll pull out at daylight!"

"Didn't say you were unwelcome, did I?" Tim's tone was frosty.

"You didn't need to," Doc reminded him. "Everything was fine until Chuck told you who we are. You don't like the Sound Logging Company, do you?" he demanded shrewdly.

"Why should I?" Tim demanded with some heat. "We're a chin-whisker outfit of hand-loggers," he went on with a touch of bitterness. "Every pirate in these waters steals our timber. Nobody dares touch a stick of the Sound Logging Company, because of your

25

fancy log patrol! We're too poor to pay for that sort of protection. Only the big companies can afford it.

"Your outfit doesn't care what happens to us," he went on. "If we're put out of business, it means less competition for you. Maybe you'll get a chance to buy our timber for half what it's worth! Why should we love a giant like that?"

"What's wrong with giants?" Chuck demanded. "If you're hinting that my father is to blame for your troubles—"

"Easy!" Doc broke in. "No use jumping the gun. Let's change the subject." Abruptly he asked Tim, "You said you hoped to return to school this fall. Do you play football?"

The unexpectedness of the question took Tim aback for a moment. Then he shrugged, almost contemptuously. "Football? No time for such nonsense! I've been doing a man's job since I was twelve. Football!" he repeated scornfully.

Chuck stared at Doc in wonderment. What was the latter cooking up? Chuck had a lot of respect for the wiry, slender quarterback with the quick-trigger mind, but to switch the conversation to such a subject as football at this moment hardly seemed to make sense.

But Doc did not appear to be disturbed by Tim's manner. "Football is only a game," he agreed, "yet Chuck and I think it's a lot of fun. Anyway," he continued, sizing up Tim as though for the first time, "you probably couldn't play it well even if you liked it. You've got a good-looking pair of hands," he conceded. "They're big and muscular enough to throw a good pass. But you probably can't run worth a cent. Sorry I mentioned the subject!"

Tim glowered, his face flushed. "I can run a hundred yards in eleven seconds wearing these logger's boots!" he declared.

Doc's eyes widened as though in surprise. "That so?" he asked. "I'd never have believed it!" But a moment later he insisted, "Even so, football is a pretty rough game. Easy for a fellow to get hurt. You wouldn't like that!"

Tim's features went stormy. "If you think—" he began. Then stopped. "Aw, what's the use!" he exclaimed disgustedly. "I'm going home!"

He turned away, the dog trailing him. Just before darkness swallowed both of them he flung over his shoulder, "I'll be back by tomorrow noon at the latest. If you've pulled out by then, it'll suit me fine!" Then he and Kamooks vanished, following what apparently was a trail leading through the timber to the opposite side of the island.

There was a long silence, broken at last by Chuck. "Doc," he asked, "what was the idea? You rubbed it into that kid pretty hard. Didn't make sense to me."

"Sorry," Doc apologized, with mock gravity, "that my innocent motives seem so foggy to you. Maybe I wanted to get him interested in football. He's probably in perfect condition—strong as a horse and tough as a fir knot. With a couple of clunks like ourselves to run interference, he'd go for a touchdown almost every time he was given the ball!"

27

"What of it?" Chuck demanded. "He doesn't even go to our school. He may not even return to his own school, unless, as he says, he gets his summer's logging done. Besides, you deliberately tried to make him sore!"

"Did I?" Doc sounded astonished. "Well, well!"

But Chuck was not deceived by his friend's manner. "All right," he retorted. "What's the answer? You have the glimmering of a plan. Come on, Brains! Give!"

Doc yawned. "Too late," he replied. "Let's go to bed. We'd better get all the rest we can, before we have to quit this cove. I've a hunch, Mr. Harmon, that our welcome is wearing mighty thin! When Tim comes back, he may be on the warpath."

Nor would he explain further. A few moments later both boys were snuggled in their sleeping bags, now fully dried out after being drenched in the storm. Chuck was tired after the excitement of the day, yet it seemed to him that slumber was far-off. There were so many things about the situation which were puzzling that his thoughts kept drowsiness away.

Doc's apparently mysterious attitude was one of them. It was odd that he had purposely stirred Tim's anger. There must be a sound purpose behind it, for Doc never did things aimlessly. Was he cooking up some new variation of Play Twenty-Two?

Tim himself was hard to understand. In some ways he seemed to be grown-up, as if boyhood were behind him; in others he acted like a boy who had never had a chance to do the things that really interested him.

28

Play football, for instance. It was hard to believe that he actually considered the game too childish; his manner probably was a pose. For just a moment he had lowered his guard, let them see his true self, when he complained that he didn't have the time needed to spend a summer camping and exploring the islands as Chuck and Doc planned to do. Despite the grown-up ways he affected, *that* was the very thing he wanted!

Instead, he was embittered by the thought that he must keep on fighting a losing battle against log pirates—parasites that prey on the weak, not the strong. No wonder he hated the Sound Logging Company, which was rich enough to afford the protection offered by the regular patrol, which had fast boats that could overtake any thief bold enough to tamper with the company's big rafts of valuable logs. Tim might be fair-minded enough to see that neither Chuck nor Doc, although their fathers were officials of the huge timber concern, could be blamed for the situation; yet he must feel that their family loyalty naturally put them on the side of the opposition. At least, it must seem to him, they couldn't be friends unless they were in sympathy with him and his grandfather. To his way of thinking they were no more than neutrals in this log war.

And Doc, with unexpected thoughtlessness, had set out to stir Tim's anger and make it worse. The situation seemed hopeless, and Chuck decided that he'd feel better when they had put miles between themselves and Skookum-Chuck Island.

Then, abruptly, he came fully awake. Something cold and moist had touched his cheek. He opened his eyes to see the grayness of coming daylight. Then he saw, standing almost over him, the big wolf-dog, Kamooks, and knew that it was the touch of the dog's nose which had roused him.

He heard Tim's voice, harsh and commanding, "Get up! I'm taking you to Gramps!"

Chuck sat up, and saw that Doc was also sitting up in his sleeping bag. Tim stood a few paces off, the pike pole gripped in both hands. Kamooks, too, seemed on the alert, as though waiting orders from his master.

The boys pulled themselves out of their sleeping bags, and stood erect. A thin fog lay over the cove, and the air had a dank rawness. Doc said complainingly to Tim, "What's the rush? Told you we'd be out of here before noon. Might at least have let us sleep until sunup!"

Chuck also felt aggrieved. It wasn't pleasant to be awakened out of sound sleep in this fashion—a big wolf-dog sticking his cold nose against one's cheek, while somebody stood by with a sharp pike pole in readiness. He had half expected Tim Elliott would return, as Doc had predicted, and perhaps on the warpath, too. But this was carrying matters too far.

He was on the point of protesting when Tim ordered, "Don't stop to pack! Just pull on your clothes. We're hitting the trail!"

Chuck remarked defiantly, "Seems like you're running things with a high hand. Just where are we going? And what becomes of our outfit, if we leave it behind? Somebody could steal it, as well as our boat and motor!"

"It will be safe enough," Tim answered. To Kamooks, he said "Guard!"

The wolf-dog understood. With lifted hackles he moved slowly about the camp, growling softly. It was clear that nothing about camp would be touched until his master gave the word.

But Chuck wouldn't admit that he was impressed. "You said you were taking us to Gramps," he told Tim. "That isn't enough. Maybe we don't leave here until we know just what is in your mind!"

A fleeting grin crossed Tim's face. "Gramps said to fetch you," he replied. "You have the choice of coming, or staying here and trying to argue Kamooks into letting you pack up your outfit and leave. What'll it be?"

Doc eyed the dog, who seemed to be waiting for further orders. Chuck understood what was in Doc's mind. Let either of them make a move toward touching any article in camp, and the wolfish-looking Kamooks would undoubtedly attack.

"Chuck," Doc declared resignedly, "Mr. Elliott has made his point—and a very good one it is, too! I vote we go along with him, just as he says. What else can we do?"

3 ... Decision

They moved away through the dew-wet woods—
Tim Elliott leading, Chuck at his heels, and Doc
trailing. As they left the cove and began climbing the
wooded hogback, following a narrow, hard-trodden
path, Chuck turned for a look at their camp. He saw
the big wolf-dog sitting on his haunches, watching
but making no attempt to follow. Evidently Kamooks
understood that until his master and these strangers
returned, the camp and outfit must be guarded.
Chuck decided that the dog would do the job well.

The boys strode along in silence; Chuck felt there
was no use in asking questions. Tim had merely said
that he was taking them to his grandfather; he hadn't
said why, and probably he had no intention of explaining.

But the situation was interesting. What manner of
man was Gramps, otherwise called "High Explosive"? Chuck told himself there was nothing to worry
about; he and Doc hadn't done anything to offend

the owner of Skookum-Chuck, but had become his uninvited guests when driven ashore by the storm. Now they were willing to leave the place as soon as possible.

Yet Tim Elliott's apparent bitterness toward the Sound Logging Company might easily be shared by his grandfather. Chuck hadn't forgotten that Tim acted as though the Sound Logging Company was in a sense a sort of ally of the log pirates. Was it possible that this enmity extended to the boys because they were sons of officials of the big timber concern? This hardly seemed probable, yet Chuck had the uneasy feeling that he couldn't be sure. He wondered what Doc thought about it, but the latter, trudging silently at the rear, was no more communicative than the boy carrying the sharp pike pole who walked ahead.

The trail twisted through the woods and climbed steeply. At the summit, finally, Tim did not pause, but Chuck turned for a last look behind. The cove was now hidden by fog. Doc stared at him, raised his eyebrows, and shrugged. Probably Doc was also mystified. What had begun as an ordinary vacation trip among the San Juan Islands had already taken an unusual twist, and the outcome could not be foreseen. There wasn't much either of them could do except wait and see what would happen. Tim started down the ridge, and the boys followed him without a word.

Now they were moving through a stand of big timber—Douglas fir that was hundreds of years old and which would make prime logs. To Chuck this forest

33

was more than "just trees." His father was a timber-man, and that was what he, too, hoped to be. Doc had the same ambition. They'd planned to take a full forestry course when they entered college. Later, they'd work for Sound Logging Company.

This island timber was highly valuable; no wonder log pirates were willing to risk arrest in order to steal it. This forest meant a living for Gramps and Tim, even though with crude hand-logging equipment only a small amount of the timber could be harvested each year. An outfit such as the Sound Logging Company, with its modern gear, could convert these trees into cash in almost no time. If the log pirates forced the Elliotts to quit, the Sound Logging Company probably would take over.

For the first time, Chuck felt that he saw the situation through Tim's eyes. It wasn't surprising that the boy viewed the Sound Logging Company, and every person connected with it, suspiciously. For all he knew to the contrary, the presence of Chuck and Doc on Skookum-Chuck Island might be part of a plan to seize the timber. He had only their word that they had landed on Skookum-Chuck because of the storm, after being fired upon by the Jarvis gang.

"We're nearly there," Tim announced at last. Chuck guessed they had walked at least a mile after leaving the cove. The three swung around a rocky shoulder on the mountainside, and ahead and below Chuck glimpsed a flat-roofed cabin built of logs, just back from the shore of a lagoon. Jutting into the water in front of the cabin was a floating wharf, and moored to it was a skiff. Smoke rose from the cabin chimney, but otherwise there was no sign of life about the place.

"Gramps is waiting," Tim went on. "He's been watching us ever since we crossed over the ridge!"

Again Chuck had a feeling of suppressed excitement, as though something was going to happen. It seemed impossible to him that anybody at the cabin could have seen movement along the trail up on the thickly wooded side of the ridge, yet Tim had said it was so. As though reading Chuck's thoughts the strange boy added, "Gramps and I keep our eyes peeled so that none of the Jarvis gang can slip up on us from behind, during daylight. Kamooks watches things at night. Jarvis has tried twice to burn us out!"

A moment later they were walking across a small clearing, and Tim waved his hand and called out, "Hi, Gramps!" Chuck looked ahead at the cabin. Framed in the single window were the head and shoulders of an old man. The fingers of his right hand were gripped about the dull-glinting barrel of a rifle. Not only, Chuck realized, had the three of them been watched as they came down the mountainside, but he and Doc had been covered by the old man's gun.

Tim leaned his pike pole against the outside of the cabin, and opened the door. He walked in, and the other boys followed. "I brought 'em, Gramps!" he announced, then stepped aside. Standing there in the center of the log-walled room, Chuck and Doc stared around in curiosity, and perhaps a little apprehensively.

The room was quite large. At the opposite end was a wide, stone fireplace, a pile of burning fir knots within it, for the night had been cool. The fire cast a reddish glow in the room, which would otherwise have been dark and gloomy, for there was only one other small window aside from the one at which the old man sat.

The floor was uneven, and seemed to Chuck that its solid-looking planks had been split by hand from straight-grained cedar logs; the cabin itself was the work of a clever ax-man, for in the corners each log had been carefully notched into place. There was a large rug of Indian design spread on the floor, and smaller rugs of the same pattern were hung on the walls. But other than a few handmade chairs, the rest of the room was barren. Its interior was smoke-stained, and had signs of long usage.

One door led to what was probably a bedroom, another to a small kitchen.

But these minor details held Chuck's attention only for a brief moment. His eyes went to the old man seated by the window, and he knew that Doc was also studying the owner of Skookum-Chuck Island.

Tim's grandfather sat in a big chair built of peeled alder saplings which had been fitted together with great care. Dressed in the same rough sort of clothing that Tim wore, he leaned back in the chair, one knobby hand resting on the worn, smooth-polished wood. the other still gripping the gun barrel. There

36

was a footrest which supported his legs in a fashion as though he had no control over them—and Chuck remembered Tim had said that Gramps would never walk again.

But otherwise, despite his advanced age, he looked like a man who still possessed considerable strength; a big man, too, judging by the way his gaunt frame filled the chair. He had thick, white hair, bushy eyebrows, a white mustache which drooped at the ends. From beneath the overhanging brows, gray eyes that were bright as an eagle's peered intently at the boys.

Chuck had the feeling that there was X-ray power in those eyes, for the gaze of the old man seemed to penetrate him through and through. Chuck decided that the name "High Explosive" had not been misplaced so far as Tim's grandfather was concerned, a man with short-fused temper who was easily aroused, and probably legendary among old-time loggers when he had been at the peak of his strength. Yet at the same time Chuck felt no hostility in the old man's gaze; rather it was one of curiosity, and when he spoke at last his voice was almost gentle.

"Which one of you," he asked, "is named Harmon?"

Chuck took a deep breath and replied, "I'm Chuck Harmon, sir."

Old "H.E." grunted. "Guessed as much," he declared. "You got the look of a Harmon." He paused, and added, "Take after your grandpap. Same breed of cats."

"You knew my grandfather, sir?" Chuck asked

with interest. He wasn't sure that the old man felt friendly toward him. Yet the remark about Chuck's grandfather stirred the boy's curiosity. The grandfather had died before Chuck was born, yet the boy had always been fascinated with stories of his strength and exploits. "Bull," as he had been nicknamed, had been a tradition among old-time loggers. He had been a rugged, courageous timberman of the old school, and Chuck liked to believe that, in some ways at least, Bull Harmon wouldn't have been ashamed of his own grandson.

"I knew him," replied Gramps shortly. "Too well, I reckon! We were partners once, but we busted up. Guess each of us was too fond of having his own way. Still, I always figured he got the upper hand of me. If it hadn't been for that, I'd own half of Sound Logging Company today!"

Chuck straightened up in protest. The old man seated in the chair seemed to be hinting that Grandfather Harmon was a tricky sort of individual. Chuck's family loyalty wouldn't permit that statement to go unchallenged.

"I don't know what you mean, sir," he replied stiffly, "but whatever happened between you and my grandfather I'm sure was no fault of his, and I'm likewise sure that he was right!"

Gramps stared at him moodily. At last he shrugged. "I won't argue," he declared. "It happened long ago. Anyway, it's over and done with now."

But Tim was unwilling to let the matter drop there.

38

"I know the story," he broke in. "Bull Harmon bought your share of Sound Logging Company because you needed money in a hurry. After you paid your debts, you took what money was left and bought Skookum-Chuck, so that my father would have a start. I've heard you tell about it a dozen times—"

"You hush up!" Gramps interrupted. "What's done is done!"

"I still insist my grandfather was right, whatever he did," Chuck said. "If you're trying to make out that he acted dishonestly," and he glowered at Tim, "I'll back up what I'm saying!"

Tense silence gripped the room. There was an odd expression on Doc's face—half-amused, half-alarmed. But the tension was broken by a chuckle from the old man at the window.

"Spunky!" he declared. "I like that. Now I *know,*" he addressed Chuck, "that you're a real Harmon. Spunk runs in your family, seems like.

"Well," he added with a touch of pride, "it runs in mine, too!" His gaze rested on Tim approvingly. "But," he continued, "there's no need for you two young roosters to start rufflin' your feathers at each other. Tim, I reckon you know what I want you to do!"

Tim hesitated only a second. Then he nodded. A shy smile crossed his face for a moment as he stepped toward Chuck and offered the latter his hand. Chuck, surprised and pleased at this turn of events, grinned and took Tim's hand. Suddenly the atmosphere became more congenial.

Gramps nodded satisfaction. "I've had my curiosity settled," he said. "That's the only reason I wanted Tim to fetch you here. Just wanted to see if Bull Harmon's grandson took after him. Reckon he does!"

Abruptly his manner changed. He waved a gnarled hand as though in dismissal. "You two best be on your way! Tim said you're headin' for Orcas. If you don't hustle, the fog will trap you here. She's thickenin' now. Always does after a storm.

"Tim and I," he concluded, "have work to do. You boys are on your vacation. There's no such thing as a vacation on Skookum-Chuck! So long, now."

But Chuck did not stir. He stood there a long moment, as though thinking. Then it happened. Of a sudden he heard his own voice saying, "Maybe, sir, we're not going to Orcas, unless you order us to leave this island!" He couldn't have explained why he said it. Almost it seemed to him that some invisible presence stood by his side, telling him what to say.

Gramps stared hard at him. "What's that?"

"I said, sir," Chuck replied firmly, "that we're not leaving just now, unless you tell us we have to go!"

The bristly white brows of the old man drew together as he regarded Chuck in puzzled fashion. Tim and Doc likewise seemed surprised. Then Gramps spoke, an odd tone in his words.

"You've got somethin' on your mind, boy," he urged. "Let's have it!"

Chuck took a deep breath as his mind groped for the right words. Out of nowhere the impulsive thought had come, but now its purpose was clearer. Perhaps it had been prompted by what Gramps had said concerning his break-up with Bull Harmon— the inference that Gramps had been unfairly treated. If it hadn't been for that split, he might still have been half-owner of Sound Logging Company, whereas all he and Tim had now was this little island for which they must fight a losing battle against log pirates. Or it might have been that Chuck was resentful over that rifle bullet with which the Jarvis gang had answered the appeal for help made by Doc and himself. Bull Harmon wouldn't have overlooked a thing like that! Either one of these things, or maybe a combination of the two, had aroused his desire to help the Elliotts.

"Say on, boy!" Gramps exclaimed impatiently.

"Doc and I have our motorboat," Chuck replied. "Tim told us of the trouble he has, with only a skiff and a pair of oars, in patrolling the island against these log pirates. We'd like to help out. Isn't that right, Doc?"

Doc said, "Huh?" His eyebrows went up in astonishment. Apparently he hadn't been expecting this sort of thing at all. Yet he was quick-witted, and he recovered his poise quickly. "Sure," he agreed, but without any apparent enthusiasm. "Sounds like a swell idea." He swallowed a couple of times.

Gramps stared at Chuck in undisguised amazement. Tim also looked surprised—yet pleased.

"You mean," Gramps asked in rather an awed voice, "that you're willin' to use your motorboat to set up a log patrol of our own? You want to bite off a hunk of our trouble?"

Chuck smiled. "That's it! Our boat is a lot faster than Tim's skiff. The engine has a fifteen-horsepower rating. It will even be useful to tow log rafts to the cove on the other side of the island. I think our boat is even faster than Jarvis' tug. With it we can keep watch on all sides of the island so that no pirates can steal your logs without our discovering it in time."

Silence came again. Chuck and the others waited for Gramps' reply. It came at last, with a queer note in his voice.

"Never heard the beat of it!" he exclaimed softly, almost to himself. He thought of it a moment longer, and wagged his head as though in disbelief.

But suddenly his manner changed, became almost stiff. "Bull Harmon and I used to be friends," he pointed out. "We'd fight for each other at the drop of a peavey. Yet we had a big quarrel, and he wound up by getting Sound Logging Company, while all I have left is Skookum-Chuck Island. You're Bull Harmon's grandson. Sure you ain't makin' this offer just because you feel sorry for Tim and me?"

These Elliotts were a proud clan, Chuck realized. Well, he told himself, he liked that! But it was easy to see why Gramps would be suspicious. Old H.E.— or High Explosive—wasn't the type of man who would be quick to beg a favor. Particularly of anybody named Harmon!

"Of course not, sir!" Chuck assured him. "I hope I'm not that foolish. The point is that Doc and I have become interested in this fight you and Tim are making. We'd like to see you win, and we believe you can, if you can stop Jarvis from stealing your logs."

The old man nodded, as though satisfied. "What about your vacation?" he asked. "It'll take time to cut logs and sell 'em. Jarvis will be watchin' us night and day."

"Doc and I," Chuck assured him, "would have more fun running our log patrol than we would if we spent the summer loafing on Orcas. Good experience for us, too. We're going to be timbermen ourselves, some day. Isn't that right, Doc?"

The latter blinked. "Sure," he agreed rather flatly. Chuck had him puzzled. This wasn't the way the two of them usually operated. Doc liked to figure out the team's play. Now Chuck apparently wanted to call the signals and carry the ball at the same time! Well, Doc reminded himself resignedly, he'd have to go along with Chuck, of course; loyalty to his pal wouldn't permit him to do anything else.

Gramps shook his head doubtfully. "Seems like you youngsters don't know what you're gettin' into," he said. "Maybe you hadn't thought that there can be plenty of danger ahead. This Jarvis gang won't stop at anything!"

"We realize that, sir," Chuck answered, thinking of that rifle bullet fired from the tug. "But we're willing to risk it, aren't we, Doc?"

Doc gulped, but made no reply. He wasn't scared; nobody had ever questioned his courage successfully. The point was that he was disturbed by Chuck's

43

eagerness to get into this fight. Of one thing he was certain: he and Chuck were going to talk this over in detail at the first opportunity!

Gramps faced his grandson. "What do you say, boy?" he asked.

"Whatever you decide suits me, Gramps," Tim replied. "Maybe we don't need help. We've got along without help so far; maybe we can keep on."

"Trouble is," Gramps reminded him, "we're not gettin' anywhere. We're losin' our logs almost as fast as they can be cut. If we only had money, so we could pay the regular log patrol folks— But, shucks! No use talkin' about *that!*"

"There's a way by which you can pay us, Mr. Elliott," remarked Doc suddenly. As in the case of Chuck, the idea had come to Doc out of nowhere.

"What's that?" Gramps demanded sharply.

"Tim told us that he'd probably have to quit school," Doc went on rapidly. "If we helped patrol this island, so that these pirates couldn't steal your logs, then Tim could finish school, couldn't he?"

"Reckon so," was the old man's comment. "But what has that got to do with payin' you boys?"

Doc grinned at Chuck, and winked. Then to Gramps he said, "Maybe Tim could transfer to our school in Seattle," he explained. "That means he could play football. He has the finest hands I've ever seen on a passer. Still," he added as though he had just remembered, "he told us once that he didn't think much of football!"

Gramps snorted. "He said that? Shucks! Must

44

have been foolin'. Fact is, he's crazy about the game. Durin' the football season he doesn't talk about anything else. That right, Tim?"

The latter appeared embarrassed. His face reddened, and he admitted, "Maybe I've talked a little about it—at times."

Chuck grinned. He was proud of Doc. It seemed to Chuck that he understood now why Doc apparently had gone to some trouble to irritate Tim on the subject of football; the canny quarterback hoped that by getting Tim aroused sufficiently, the Skookum-Chuck boy might want to play the game. Now Gramps had bared the fact that Tim was already a football player at heart.

Gramps wagged his head again in bewildered fashion. "Never heard the beat of it!" he declared. "You two youngsters willin' to spoil your vacation just so Tim can have a chance he might never have. Makes me think there's a little good left in this world after all."

Yet he cleared his throat ominously, and looked away from Tim, as though trying to avoid the latter's gaze. "Sorry, boys," he announced, "but it's too risky. Can't let you do it, even though I know what it could mean to Tim. Even though Bull Harmon and I broke up years ago, I couldn't live with myself if I had to remember the rest of my years that I brought harm to his grandson. What would your folks say?" and he looked at both Chuck and Doc.

"We intend to write and tell them what we are doing," Chuck answered promptly. "Our parents are in Alaska for the summer; Doc's father and mine are planning to build a pulp mill near Ketchikan, and our mothers went along for the trip. They've let Doc and me have the summer to ourselves.

"We'll tell them, of course, but I know what my father's answer will be, and I'm sure Doc's father will feel the same way. They'll tell us to go ahead. They don't like log pirates any better than you do!"

Gramps' whiskered face split in a grin. "Blamed if you don't even *talk* like a Harmon!" he declared approvingly. "Good loggers have to stick together. That's what Bull Harmon and myself used to say when the goin' got tough!"

"Then you'll agree, Gramps?" Tim asked eagerly.

The old man frowned. "Didn't say so, did I?" he retorted. But at the stricken look that came into Tim's face, he added, "Reckon it means a lot to you, doesn't it?"

Tim nodded.

"Seems like all three of you have got me in a corner," Gramps complained. "If I thought there'd be any real danger, I'd still say no. But Lem Jarvis is such a coward that I reckon he'll keep clear of the island as soon as he finds out we've set up a patrol of our own. And if he doesn't have a chance to steal our logs, we'll have money in the bank before fall comes, enough money to let Tim go to school in Seattle. Be lonesome for me, of course, but Kamooks will be company. And Tim can come home durin' vacations, and maybe on week ends now and then."

He held up his hand commandingly, as though to

46

halt any outburst of enthusiasm over his decision. "Get started, then!" he ordered. "Tim, see that the boys get breakfast; then bring their boat and outfit around the island to our lagoon. You'll have to hustle," he concluded, "before the fog gets too thick."

Once the decision had been made, little time was lost. Breakfast was a hasty yet ample meal, and soon the three boys were climbing the mountainside on their way back to the camp in the cove. Tim was jubilant, more talkative than usual, as he led the way along the trail. They crossed the ridge at last, and began moving downward through the timber. At least two hours had elapsed since they had left the camp under guard of the big wolf-dog.

The fog had become so dense that even when they were within a hundred yards of the camp they could not see the place. For no reason which he could have given, Chuck felt a twinge of uneasiness. Perhaps Tim felt the same way, for he quickened his pace as they neared the cove. No sound broke the stillness. Then they were within a few paces of the camp, and Tim called questioningly in a low voice, "Kamooks?"

They heard the dog whine in reply, and then Chuck could make out the place, the shadowy shape of the wooden disks standing in a ring about the spot where they had spent the night. Just beyond was the outboard-powered skiff, glistening with drops of wet mist. Everything seemed all right, he told himself in relief!

Yet Tim gave an exclamation and plunged ahead. From behind one of the upright cookies the wolf-dog dragged himself, whining in pain. The next moment Tim was bent over him, hands exploring the dog's body in search of injuries.

There was a long, gaping wound on the dog's left shoulder. Tim pointed to it, and said in a strange voice, "The point of a pike pole did that! Jarvis and his gang have been here!"

4 ... The Plan

Kamooks was hurt, badly, but aside from that gash on his shoulder, he seemed to have no other wounds. Chuck and Doc stared around, as though half expecting to see Jarvis or some of his men emerge from the fog. But the log pirates—and surely nobody else could have been here—were gone.

About the camp the damp sand was scored by many foot marks, the prints of heavy boots. There had been a battle here. Tim stood up, and his eyes quickly read the story of what had taken place.

He pointed to a V-shaped trench in the sand, at the edge of the water. "They landed there in a skiff," he explained. "Because of the fog they didn't see Kamooks or the camp. But when they came ashore, he challenged 'em! Somebody jabbed him with a pike pole, but he fought 'em back into their skiff. Probably they figured I must be near, so they didn't stop long enough to take any logs. For all they knew, I was close by with Gramps' rifle!"

He bent down impulsively and hugged the dog. "Good boy, Kamooks!" he exclaimed, his voice choked. "You saved my logs this time. Now we'll get you home in a hurry, so Gramps can fix your wound. He'll know what to do."

He turned to Chuck. "Will your outboard work?" he asked.

Chuck nodded. "We cleaned and dried it after we made camp," he told Tim. "Ought to fire the first time. But I'll find out."

He climbed into the skiff and went aft. The change of the tide had left the water depth in the cove at almost exactly the same stage as when they had arrived the previous day. Nevertheless, he tipped the motor forward until the propeller was clear of the water; then he spun the flywheel. The engine sputtered a little, but immediately began firing smoothly. He let it run for a few moments, then shut it off.

Then he clambered out of the skiff, and with Doc's help shoved the boat almost clear of the beach. Tim stooped and picked up Kamooks easily enough, although the dog probably weighed more than a hundred pounds, and carried him to the skiff, easing him down in the bow. Doc and Chuck were busy gathering their outfit, stowing it amidships. When everything was loaded, Tim shoved the boat clear, jumped into it, and settled down beside his dog.

To Chuck at the stern he said, "Turn right when you clear the mouth of the cove, and stay as close to shore as you can. We've got to keep it in sight all the time, if we can. If we don't we're likely to wander off in the fog and get lost."

With his hand on the wound starter rope, Chuck asked, "What if Jarvis' tug is waiting just outside? They'll hear the motor, and they may see us." He had not forgotten the ominous sound of that rifle bullet whistling past his head.

"Not likely," Tim replied. "They've probably pulled out for the time being, and won't be back until they're sure that Kamooks is gone. Fog doesn't bother Jarvis; he knows these islands like he knows the deck of his own tug. My guess is that he's been scared off for a few hours, maybe a few days."

Chuck nodded and jerked the starter rope. The motor roared instant response, and then the skiff began heading toward the entrance.

They moved slowly, for Chuck kept the motor throttled down; he was unfamiliar with the channel, and didn't want to pile the skiff on the rocks. But he watched Tim, who crouched in the bow, signaling with his hands which way to steer. Soon they were outside the cove, and Chuck swung right, as Tim had previously directed.

Now the motor was given full throttle, and the skiff went racing over the glassy water. Chuck, hand on the tiller, kept the boat as far offshore as he could without losing sight of land; he didn't want to get too close for fear of heading into some rocky point, for the beach was raggedly uneven. Tim likewise kept lookout, but he made no more signals, and Chuck assumed that the navigation was satisfactory, even though it seemed risky.

Doc seemed preoccupied with his thoughts, as time

53

slipped by. Sometimes he looked ahead at Tim and Kamooks in the bow. Once he looked aft and caught Chuck's gaze, and shrugged his shoulders as though saying, "What's going to happen, will happen." But mostly he watched the rugged shore swimming past in the ghostly fog.

At last Tim turned and wiggled his hand up and down, signaling Chuck to slow the motor. As the roar of the powerful little engine diminished somewhat, Tim called back to Chuck, "Take it easy now! We're almost there!" Peering shoreward, Chuck could make out the mouth of the lagoon. He estimated that the trip from the cove where Tim's logs were rafted had taken about fifteen minutes.

Soon the boat was sliding alongside the float. Doc jumped out and made it fast. Then Kamooks was lifted out by Tim, who picked up the dog again and carried him to the cabin.

Chuck was impressed by the care which Tim lavished on his pet. Kamooks seemed unable to walk, and evidently Tim feared that the point of the pike pole had broken the dog's shoulder. Rather than risk hurting Kamooks further, Tim was willing to carry him, heavy though he was.

Chuck and Doc followed Tim and his burden into the room where Gramps was waiting. The old man saw the wound on the dog's shoulder, and his face hardened. "Jarvis?" he asked Tim. The latter nodded.

"Fetch him here," Gramps commanded, "and lay him across my knees." Tim did as he had been told, and the fingers of the old man groped knowingly about the dog's body. At last he grunted as though satisfied.

"Looks like a deep stab-wound, that's all," he decided. "Kamooks was lucky. If it had been an inch or so more toward the center of his chest, he'd have been a goner. Good thing you carried him, Tim, instead of making him try to walk. Saved him a lot of pain."

He patted the dog's head consolingly. Kamooks turned and looked up at the old man, and wagged his tail feebly. Apparently the dog understood that he would be cared for now, and that everything possible would be done to help him.

"Bring everything in our medicine kit," Gramps told Tim, and the latter obeyed. Gramps selected a bottle containing a dark liquid, and a piece of clean cotton. "This'll hurt him," Gramps told Tim. "Best hang onto his head. He won't bite me, of course, but he may get excited and try to get away. May hurt more than he can stand."

But Kamooks proved that he had more endurance than even Gramps suspected for, although he quivered as the burning disinfectant was applied, he did not get panicky, and as Tim stroked his head and talked consolingly to him, he even tried to lick the boy's hand.

Yet Gramps was not finished. At his direction, Tim brought a length of clean net-twine, and a long needle used for mending seines. The twine was sterilized by soaking it in the contents of the bottle. Once more

55

Tim soothed the dog, and soon the job was finished. The opening of the long and deep wound had been neatly stitched together.

"Get an old blanket and spread it before the fireplace," Gramps directed. Tim did this. Then he lifted Kamooks down, and the dog stretched gratefully before the warmth.

Gramps' face was grim as he turned to Chuck. "You see what kind of a rogue this Lem Jarvis is," he said. "Tried to kill Kamooks! Next time it might be one of us. You still want to go ahead with your plan to set up a patrol?"

"More than ever!" Chuck assured him.

"That goes for me!" Doc declared.

Gramps nodded. "Figured that's the way you'd feel," he declared. "But," he warned, "we've got to be careful. I'd rather lose everything than have one of you boys get hurt. Maybe we can outsmart Jarvis without getting into a real battle."

He looked down at the dog by the fire. "Kamooks will be up and around before long," he decided. "He'll do his part, soon as he's able to. There's enough wolf in him so that he won't forget who tried to kill him. I'd hate to be the log pirate who faces him next time!"

Gramps looked at Chuck again. "You got any plan?" he asked.

"I haven't had time to talk it over with Doc and Tim," Chuck replied, "but we can split up the patrol into four-hour watches, at least at night. Even if

56

Jarvis tried to force his way into the cove, our boat is fast enough to scoot back here and fetch help in a hurry. We'd be back at the cove with reinforcements before he could make up a raft and tow it away."

"Sounds all right," Gramps approved. "Anything is better than lettin' him help himself."

"I'll take the first watch," Chuck went on, "Doc the second, and Tim the third. But we'll need more gas if we keep it up for long. We have only a few gallons left in the reserve can we brought along, as we'd planned to get more at Orcas. Five gallons, mixed with oil, will keep us going for several days."

"I'll get it," Tim volunteered. "It's only a ten-mile row to the mainland. Besides, I want to get word to the sawmill people to send their tug to pick up what logs we have left. I can make the round trip in six hours."

"We could make the trip a lot faster in our boat," Doc pointed out, "rather than your skiff."

"It would use up just that much more gas," Tim reminded him. "I don't mind a little paddling like that; I'm used to rowing. Besides, we couldn't start the patrol right away, which may be important."

"How about this fog?" Chuck asked. "You could get lost."

Tim laughed. "I can find my way around these islands with my eyes shut," he declared. "I know all the landmarks."

"That's right," Gramps remarked. "I'm not worried about Tim." He added, "We'll buy the gas.

It's little enough we'll be doin' to repay you boys for this job." He said it in a manner to dispose of all argument.

"Best get things started," he went on. "Tim, you'll have to hustle to get back here soon after dark. Chuck, it won't do any harm to keep an eye on the cove. Let Jarvis hear your engine in the fog. He won't know what it means, and it'll keep him puzzled."

It made sense, and Chuck nodded agreement. "I'll write a letter to my father," he told Doc, "and tell him what we're doing. He'll tell your folks. Tim can mail it when he gets to the mainland. Suit you?"

"Suits me," Doc replied.

Yet it was nearing noon before things really got underway. Tim had left for the mainland, carrying the letter. Writing it, Chuck had found, wasn't as easy as he had expected; it was rather difficult to explain to his father just how he felt, but he did the best he could. "Gramps," he wrote, "seems to feel that grandfather wronged him. I know he's mistaken, of course, and maybe by helping him in this way we can change his mind. Also, Doc and I want to do what we can for Tim. He's tops, and deserves the best! We'll be careful, of course." He was sure that his father, as well as Doc's, would approve, once they understood. He hoped that they wouldn't worry . . .

He wasn't exactly worried, himself, yet he felt none too confident. Jarvis was a violent, dangerous man. Perhaps the only way to beat him was by outsmarting him, as Gramps had suggested. But it was going to take a lot of good luck to do it!

Before Tim left there had been time for him to give Chuck and Doc a better idea of the situation. So far, the hand-logging had been carried out only on the side of the island where Gramps had built his cabin. This made it easier for Tim to do the work and likewise look after the needs of his helpless grandfather. As soon as Tim had cut enough logs to make up a small raft, he had used the skiff to tow them to the cove where they would be sheltered from storms. From time to time, as he got word to the sawmill on the mainland, a tug came and towed the logs away.

But towing even a small raft of logs around the island to the cove, as Tim did, using only a skiff powered by a pair of oars, was a back-breaking task, even though he always timed it with a favorable tide. Still, it was a terrific job, and too often the result of Tim's hard work went for naught; Jarvis stole the logs.

The amazing thing, it seemed to Chuck, was that Tim—unaided since Gramps had been crippled when his legs had been pinched between two rolling logs— had been able to do such heavy work. Yet Tim had devised a rather clever way of hand-logging the steep slope.

First, he cut down the trees, three to four feet thick at the butt, by means of a narrow falling-saw, a job ordinarily requiring two men because the blade is so limber that it cannot be held level by one man. To avoid this, he drove a forked stick several feet long into the ground on the opposite side of the tree trunk.

Then he fastened a length of rawhide from the top of the forked stick to the free end of his saw. In this way the blade was kept level by the rawhide strip and the end of the stick which swayed back and forth with each stroke of the saw.

Once the tree had crashed to earth, Tim had figured out an ingenious way of getting it down the mountain and into salt water. Taking a turn around the trunk with the cable, he anchored the fallen tree to the trunk so that it would not slide down the hill. With his double-bitted ax he lopped off all limbs, until he had a bare stick more than a hundred feet long. As he had been careful to drop the tree with its top pointing downward, all that was necessary to do now was to sharpen the small tip, or upper end, cover it with heavy grease, then, after the cable was free, by means of a peavey work the point of the stick free until the force of gravity took over. Point downward, the long stick would go sliding down the slope and stop only when it had reached the water. Thereafter, it could be "bucked," or cut up into regular saw-logs thirty-two feet long.

But it was dangerous work! It took courage. "That boy," Doc whispered to Chuck in an awed voice, "isn't afraid of *anything!* What a football player *he'll* make!" Yet it was doubtful that Tim Elliott would ever have his chance on a gridiron.

The fog had thickened until it had become a wet, grayish curtain that limited visibility to no more than a few yards. But Tim, rowing the skiff, had set off as confidently as though in brilliant sunshine. There seemed no reason to worry as to whether or not he could find his way to the mainland and back. He had spent all his life among these islands, and he knew his way around.

Chuck and Doc had reached agreement as to how they would maintain the patrol. Chuck would take the first watch, while Doc would remain at the cabin with Gramps. Other than that they had no definite plan. All that seemed necessary was to let Jarvis discover that the logs in the cove were being watched. Yet before Chuck put off in the powered skiff, Gramps uttered a final word of caution.

"You be plenty careful, boy," the old man told him. "Jarvis may be smarter than we think. It won't be long before he knows all about what we're up to. Then we'll have to be on guard!"

"I'll be careful, sir," Chuck replied, and meant it. Playing tag with a gang of log pirates who had a rifle and probably would not hesitate to use it, was a dangerous game. The thought still was in his mind as, with the motor firing perfectly, he headed out of the lagoon and began retracing the route taken earlier when Kamooks had been brought home.

This time he did not run at full speed, for the reason that Tim wasn't along to help him keep away from rocks hidden in the fog, and likewise it was necessary to conserve gas until Tim brought back a fresh supply from the mainland. He held the boat close inshore, for it would be easy to go astray if he lost sight of land. He kept on for more than a quarter of an hour, and nothing happened, and by now he was certain that he wasn't far from the cove where the logs were rafted.

It seemed time to wait and watch, and he shut off the motor, letting the craft drift slowly along with the tide, which was running in the same direction that he was headed.

With the purring roar of the motor no longer in his ears, the silence that came was almost ominous. At intervals he heard the complaining cries of sea gulls, as though the thick mist interfered with their search for food. Far-off he could hear the occasional hooting of an ocean-going steamer as it groped its way through the fog. He had read that sound carries a remarkable distance under such conditions. It wasn't possible to guess where Jarvis and his men had gone, but so far as Chuck knew, they were nowhere near, or at least their tug wasn't underway, or he believed he would have heard the sound of its engine.

Yet it seemed best for him to keep quiet while he did a bit of scouting. He unshipped the oars, and began rowing slowly and as silently as possible, still close to shore and headed toward the mouth of the cove.

Despite his care, the oarlocks creaked a little with every stroke. Yet it was a sound which would not carry far. The trouble was that he didn't know if Jarvis' tug was near! If the log pirates had heard him, and were purposely keeping quiet, there was a chance that he might row into a trap.

Yet as time passed he heard nothing alarming nor

saw anything at all save the rocky shore, indistinct in the mist. The tide helped carry him along. By and by there came to his ears the soft swishing of the tidal current lapping the edge of the rocky beach. This must be the cove.

He swung closer inshore, then stopped rowing and listened. He was about to resume stroking with his oars when he heard a sharp metallic clank, and the sound gave him a nervous start. Some craft was out there in the fog, and not far away, either. As he listened intently he heard other sounds—a light splash, a bump as of wood striking wood. Almost as though the thick, wet curtain had been stripped aside, he could guess what the noise meant.

Jarvis' tug was hove-to off the mouth of the cove, and some of his men were getting ready to go ashore in their skiff, apparently to reconnoiter the situation. If they found nobody on guard, they'd steal another batch of logs. Obviously they hadn't been scared off too much by the clash with Kamooks; and, too, they might have heard the motorboat when it pulled out. Hearing nothing further of it, they had guessed that nobody had been left on watch. But they had waited long enough to be sure; now they were moving in.

Chuck rested on his oars, debating what to do. In a sense he felt trapped, for he could now see the mouth of the cove, and knew that he was between it and the tug. He could start his motor and make a dash for it, but the log pirates would quickly understand what was happening. Once he was gone, they'd hurriedly take what logs they could, make a raft of them,

63

secure a towline to it, and disappear in the mist before he could fetch any possible help. The best way to beat them was by a trick.

He began rowing again, as quietly as possible yet swiftly, too, straight toward the mouth of the cove.

Between strokes he could hear the skiff of the log pirates also getting underway—the splash of oars, the thump of them now and then against the gunwale of their skiff, for the pirates seemed sure enough that they had not been detected, as they were careless about making noise. He could even hear them talking, but he couldn't see their skiff and couldn't tell how many men were in it. The tug itself, of course, was also hidden.

But their noise served to cover any sound he made, and he rowed faster, passing through the narrow, rocky entrance which he and Doc had been lucky to find the previous day. He kept on until Tim's raft appeared; then he oared the skiff parallel to the logs until he was at the farthest end of the cove. Then he shipped his oars, wound the starter rope around the motor's flywheel, and set himself to wait.

There was a chance, of course, that the men in the skiff would discover that he was alone and, assuming that he was unarmed, drive ahead in an attempt to capture him. If that happened, he decided, he could probably reach the shore in time to take to the woods. It wouldn't stop them from stealing the logs, however. He had to risk discovery before making his play. The worst thing that could happen would be for the fog to lift, but the air was quiet after the storm, and it would take a strong wind to blow the mist away.

As he waited, he heard them coming. Now they were through the entrance, and if they came much closer it was possible that they would see him. He guessed they'd have the rifle with them this time, with the idea in mind that if the wolf-dog was still on guard, they'd finish him off with a shot. Chuck waited awhile longer, then gave a yank on the starter rope.

The motor thundered instant response. He gunned it, and in the small cove the roar of it became almost deafening. Several times he throttled it down, then turned on full power. To the men in the skiff it must have sounded as though the craft was getting up momentum to go charging at them. Abruptly he throttled until the engine barely purred. He wanted to hear what they were doing. His bluff was going to have to work, or the outcome would be disastrous.

5 ... Jarvis Strikes Back

here were confused sounds at the entrance of the
cove. He guessed that the log pirates in the skiff
were thoroughly alarmed, and were determined to
get back to the tug before they were overtaken. For
all they knew to the contrary, a boatload of armed
men was already in pursuit of them. He could hear
their oars flailing as they pulled out of the cove and
headed back for the protection of the tug.

Chuck grinned in triumph, and gunned the motor
to speed them along. The next instant he regretted it,
for something skittered over the water a few feet
from his skiff. Twice more it happened, and he knew
they were firing blindly in his direction. They
couldn't see him, of course, but they could hear his
motor, and were guessing rather accurately where he
was located. Quickly he shut off the motor, but not
before he had shot the skiff a hundred feet to the left
of where he had been. There he waited in silence,
hoping that the firing had stopped.

Apparently the log pirates were content, for no more shots came. Soon he heard the bump of the skiff as it came alongside the tug. A few seconds later came the steady thud-thud of the tug's diesel. The sound continued, and the craft moved away in the fog. Chuck let out his breath in relief.

It had been a close call! But the big thing was that his ruse, made up on the spur of the moment, had succeeded. This would be cheering news for Gramps and Tim.

Yet common sense told him that the log pirates would be harder to trick next time. When Jarvis had time to think over what had happened, he would probably be prepared and on guard. One thing which seemed certain was that he wouldn't give up easily. Stealing the Elliott logs was too profitable. It would take more than mere bluff to discourage Jarvis.

But for the moment Chuck felt that he had won. He waited until he had made certain that Jarvis' tug was leaving the spot, then he started the motor and steered outward through the narrow channel.

It wasn't probable that the tug would return soon, and yet Chuck would not count on that too heavily. Jarvis was a hard man to outguess. For the remainder of his four-hour watch, Chuck kept cruising back and forth across the entrance. So far the Skookum-Chuck log patrol was working perfectly. But there was no telling how long it would be successful. Jarvis was determined, and the Elliott logs were a rich enough prize to tempt any pirate on Puget Sound.

Nothing happened, and when the time came to

head back home and turn the powerboat over to Doc, the fog was as thick as ever. Chuck wondered if Tim had made the trip to the mainland without mishap. Only a person with an instinct like that of a homing pigeon could navigate through a dense blanket such as this.

Doc, a look of relief on his face, was waiting at the float when Chuck steered the powerboat alongside. "Don't tell me what happened," Doc remarked. "Wait until Gramps can hear it, too. He's tried to act confident, but I know that he's been worried. Said more than once that he shouldn't let us get mixed up in this fight. But I think I've talked him out of *that!* I said that we were going to keep the patrol going no matter what happened—just to pay back Jarvis for shooting at us. But the reason goes deeper than that, doesn't it?"

"Tim deserves all the help we can give him," Chuck replied evasively.

Doc nodded. "So he does. But Gramps thinks that your grandfather wronged him. You'd like to change Gramps' mind, wouldn't you?"

Chuck wagged his head impatiently, a little embarrassed. "Something like that," he answered shortly, and led the way up to the cabin.

Gramps also appeared relieved. He was still seated at the window, one hand gripping the barrel of the rifle. "Reckon I've got to get used to things," he declared with a smile. "Couldn't help gettin' a little nervous when I got to thinkin' about you cruisin' along out there in the fog. Mighty easy to get lost, if a person doesn't know these waters. Any sign of the Jarvis gang?"

Chuck related what had happened. He minimized the danger, and likewise the fact that he had been scared until he was certain that the log pirates were hurrying to get away.

Gramps listened in solemn silence. "Sounds like you're holdin' back," he said finally. "Didn't they shoot at you?"

Chuck shrugged as though the fact was unimportant. "A few times," he confessed. "But, of course, they couldn't see me in the fog, and the bullets went wide."

Gramps thumped the butt of the rifle on the floor angrily. "What I'd give if I could only get around!" he complained. "I'd stand guard over those logs with this gun day and night. Next time Jarvis and his men came foolin' around, I'd get me a log pirate or two!"

But after this outburst, he became calmer. "Well," he declared resignedly, "we've won the first round, but we'll be lucky if we win the next one. Only thing we can do is keep watch and wait for him to make another move." He looked at Doc. "You be careful, boy!" he warned.

Doc nodded vigorously. "You may count on that, sir!" he assured Gramps warmly. "No log pirate is going to get within shooting distance of me, if I can help it!"

Chuck went over and patted Kamooks, who still lay by the fire. "He's doin' fine," Gramps announced.

"In a few days he'll be up and around and doin' his part, like the rest of us."

Yet Gramps was having difficulty hiding his uneasiness. "I'll be glad when Tim gets back," he remarked. "Goin' to get dark early tonight, on account of the fog. Well, now, I guess all I can do is wait."

Chuck and Doc went back to the skiff tied to the float. "So," Doc said, "you had a real brush with the Jarvis gang! More and more I'm beginning to think that we've taken on a real battle."

"What else could we have done?" Chuck asked. "If we'd closed our eyes and refused to take a hand in this, it would have seemed to be a sad vacation for us, wouldn't it? We couldn't have enjoyed ourselves."

"You're right, of course," Doc agreed. "But just the same, I think we're going to need Play Twenty-Two to win this game!"

He got into the skiff, and Chuck untied the painter and shoved the craft clear. Doc started the engine, and as the boat swung in a circle and headed back along the fog-shrouded shore, he waved his hand in farewell.

Even when the powerboat had vanished in the mist, Chuck stood there, staring in the direction it had gone and listening to the lessening sound of the motor. Doc had courage, a lot of it; also he had a nimble mind. He knew how to take care of himself. Yet Chuck could not help feeling worried. A lot of unforeseen things could happen, and probably *would* happen. Yet he had no regret over the decision he and Doc had made. Chance had pushed them into this situation; it seemed that their own self-respect demanded that they go ahead. Bull Harmon, Chuck was sure, would have done the same.

The afternoon was about gone, and the thick mist had already brought twilight. But as Chuck lingered at the float he felt a light breeze puff into the lagoon. It might be that this was no more than the breeze which usually comes up at sundown. The tide, he saw by the height of water against the piling which held the float in place, was at full flood. Sometimes the tide caused a breeze to spring up.

But if the wind strengthened, so that it blew the fog away, that could be very important. No longer would it be possible for the powerboat to operate unseen. Jarvis and his crew aboard the tug would be quick to discover that the patrol which had worried them was only a powerboat manned by an unarmed boy, and when that happened the pirates would strike quickly.

Chuck waited at the float, hoping that any minute he would hear the sound of Tim's oars as the boy returned from the mainland. But no sounds came from the fog. The noise of Doc's motor had long ago died out.

Yet the breeze continued to freshen, and the fog swirled across the lagoon. It grew darker. Rising waves splashed against the float. If another gale came before Tim returned he might be forced to find shelter on some other island. Chuck looked up at the sky and thought that he glimpsed a star. The fog was thinning, and before morning it would be gone.

He trudged slowly up to the cabin. There was no light in the living room, save the reddish glow which came from the fireplace. He saw the figure of the old man at the window. "You worried, boy?" Gramps asked.

"A little," Chuck admitted.

"So am I," Gramps declared. "A lot. I'll be glad when Tim gets back. Gettin' windy, seems to me."

Chuck settled down in front of the fireplace. Kamooks raised his head and apparently recognized the boy as a friend, for the big wolf-dog thumped his tail on the floor. After that, silence settled over the place. Chuck heard the moan of the rising wind, and he wondered how Tim was making out in that frail skiff. He wondered, too, about Doc. The wind, as near as Chuck could judge, would send waves beating against the entrance to the cove where the logs were rafted. Doc would be out there in rough water. There was always a chance that the motor would quit. He might be driven ashore, unless he could manage to hold the skiff clear by means of its oars. Jarvis and his tug probably would be abroad, particularly if the mist cleared away.

Gramps seemed to be in no mood for conversation, and likewise Chuck didn't feel much like talking. There was too much on the minds of both of them. After awhile, Chuck got up and walked outside. The fog was clearing rapidly now, and he could see stars twinkling here and there. When he came back, he discovered that Kamooks had risen and was prowling restlessly about the room. The dog appeared much stronger, thanks to the treatment Gramps had given him, and while he was still somewhat unsteady on his feet, he could walk fairly well.

"Somethin's botherin' him," Gramps remarked. "Dogs sometimes have a funny way of knowin' things that are goin' on better than most folks do."

Kamooks hobbled to the door, pushed it open, and stood there with lifted head, sniffing the wind. His ears were pricked forward, as if listening. Chuck could hear nothing save the wind, and the slap of waves against the beach in front of the cabin. After a moment Kamooks resumed his pacing.

Gramps looked at Chuck and said confidently, "Got to be patient. Everything will turn out all right." Chuck didn't reply. He could not help worrying about Tim, and certainly he was worried about Doc.

Presently he told Gramps, "I'm going down to the float. Maybe I can hear something." The old man nodded, as though he understood why the boy was troubled.

Chuck opened the door and stepped outside, Kamooks close at his heels. It was good to have the wolf-dog as company. The two of them went down the slight slope to the water, Kamooks limping behind.

Chuck looked at the sea and sky, the latter now brilliant with stars. Out beyond the mouth of the lagoon there was a chop of sizable waves, yet the wind was only a strong breeze—no storm. On his return Tim would be pulling against these whitecaps, quartering them, at least. Despite the slowness of the rowboat,

73

he should have been back before this. Still, as Gramps had said, the thing to do was to be patient.

There was no sound of Doc's motor, but this was to be expected because the wind was in the wrong quarter. He must be cruising off the cove, keeping a lookout for Jarvis' tug. No time now for the motor to start acting up, as it sometimes did. It was about time for him to be back with a report on the situation.

Chuck sat down and leaned his back against a piling which held the float in place, and Kamooks flattened beside him. It was plain now that the wolf-dog regarded him as one who rightfully belonged on Skookum-Chuck, and that was a pleasing thought. There was something about the dog's dignified manner, his obvious strength and courage, that commanded respect. He had a part to play that was just as important as that of any human being on the island.

They waited, Chuck's hand resting on the dog's head. By and by Chuck felt the dog tense. Then Kamooks raised his head as though listening. Yet Chuck could hear nothing more than the whispering of the waves.

Yet as he stared at the curling whitecaps, lighted by faint starshine from above, it seemed that one showed larger than the others, as though the water was breaking around some solid object. Kamooks whined. A few moments later Chuck heard the creak of oarlocks. He got to his feet, and presently he saw the shape of Tim's skiff moving slowly toward land.

Chuck was waiting as the craft came alongside, and he heard Tim say in a tired voice, "Almost afraid I wasn't going to make it against this wind!" Chuck wanted to say that he was amazed that Tim had managed to make headway at all, but instead he nodded as though the circumstances were usual. Tim didn't seek empty praise; he had been trained to take things as they came, and the less said about them the better.

There were two five-gallon cans of fuel aboard the skiff, and Tim handed these up to Chuck. "Told the man where I bought it," Tim explained, "that we were going to use this gas in an outboard. He mixed some oil with it, so it should work okay."

There was also a large box covered with a small tarpaulin as protection against waves splashing inboard. "Grub," Tim announced. "If we're going to log this island and run a patrol at the same time, we'll have to eat!"

He patted Kamooks' head. "You're coming along fine, boy," he told the wolf-dog. "Inside of a few days you'll be ready to fight log pirates again." Then he looked at Chuck and asked, "Anything happen while I was gone?"

Chuck told him of the near clash with Jarvis' men in the fog, and Tim smiled. "Wish I could have seen it," he remarked. "But the fog has gone, and we won't be able to play that trick on Jarvis again." He added, "About time for Doc to be back, if he relieved you four hours ago."

"He's overdue," Chuck agreed, "but I guess there's nothing to worry about. At least that's what Gramps has been telling me."

"Gramps is right," Tim declared. "Worrying doesn't help." He picked up the box of groceries and started toward the cabin, Chuck following with the cans of gasoline. As Tim pushed the door open, Gramps said almost casually, "Well, I see you made it. Figured you would, even if the wind is kickin' up. Reckon Doc will show up soon."

"If he doesn't," Tim declared, "I'm going to hike over the ridge to the cove. He might be tied up there with motor trouble."

"Not likely," Gramps replied, with the confidence of a born optimist. And a few moments later he had his faith confirmed.

Once more Kamooks grew fidgety. "Probably he hears Doc's motor," Tim interpreted. "Let's go down to the float."

Soon they heard the far-off thrumming of the outboard, rising and falling as the gusts of wind varied. Chuck felt relief. Gramps, it seemed, was right. I'll try never to worry again, Chuck promised himself. Then the powered skiff soon turned into the lagoon, and Doc shut off the engine and let the craft bump alongside the float.

He said, "Hi!" rather absently and without enthusiasm. "Give me a hand here, will you?" They saw that he was struggling with a rather large circular object lying in the bottom of the boat. Chuck recognized it as one of the cookies which had been piled around their camp at the cove—a wooden disk about four inches thick, cut from the butt of one of Tim's logs by Jarvis' men. Even in the weak light

76

Chuck could still make out the HE brand which the pirates had been so careful to remove from the stolen log.

"What are you going to do with that?" Chuck asked. "Are you collecting souvenirs?"

Doc shrugged. The disk now stood on edge on the float. "Maybe that's all it amounts to—a souvenir," he replied. "Maybe something else. Can't tell until I try out my hunch."

It was a typical answer. Chuck felt that he could read Doc's mind. Doc was at grips with an idea, and until he had proved it one way or another, he would stubbornly refuse to talk about it.

"Another Play Twenty-Two?" Chuck grinned. Again Doc shrugged, but said nothing.

Yet Tim gave an exclamation. He had rubbed his hand over the inner side of the disk. "Hey!" he cried. "That saw cut feels mighty fresh! It was done today."

He swung and faced Doc. "What about it?" he asked.

Doc nodded. "Sorry to say you're right," he replied gloomily. "Jarvis pulled a clever trick on me after dark tonight. Took another batch of your logs, Tim. I've made a mess of things!"

6 ... Trick for Trick

The three boys stood there in silence for a moment, then Doc said, "I'm mighty sorry, Tim! Guess I was sure I could outsmart Jarvis, but he made me look silly!"

"Forget it!" Tim replied. "We'll have to expect such things. He'd probably have stolen the logs anyway, even if we hadn't set up this patrol. Let's go up to the house and tell Gramps. And, don't worry about it, Doc. I know Gramps will feel the same about it as I do."

"I surely hope so!" Doc said bitterly. "But I won't blame him if he feels otherwise."

Soon they stood there in the darkened room, and perhaps Doc was glad that light from the fireplace wasn't strong enough to show his features clearly.

He didn't spare himself in telling. While cruising off the mouth of the cove, soon after the fog had lifted, he had seen the dark shape of Jarvis' tug moving slowly past the island, as if reconnoitering the

78

situation. At once he had slowed his motor and began trailing the pirate craft, careful to keep well out of easy gun range, his idea being that so long as he was in sight they wouldn't dare attempt to raid the cove.

Yet the tug seemed to be in no hurry to go any place in particular. It kept easing along, and after nearly an hour of this slow chase he began to get worried, wondering what Jarvis was up to. Finally the tug turned and headed away from the island, picking up speed so that it was soon out of sight. By no means satisfied, yet believing that his very presence had kept the pirates away from the cove, Doc turned back for a final look at the logs. Just before he reached the cove he made an alarming discovery.

Out in open water was a small raft being towed by two men rowing a skiff. His first thought was that the little raft might have come from another island, but to make sure, he sent his boat in close, slowing it so near the last logs in the raft that he was finally able to make out the brand on one of them. It consisted of two letters hooked together, but they looked like LJ. That brand could belong to one man only—Lem Jarvis! At that moment, too, he saw the pirate tug, running at full speed, bearing down on him out of the night.

There was but one thing he could do: run for it! If he lingered here he would either be cut down by the onrushing tug, or fired at. He headed for the cove. The tug swung around, picked up the skiff with the two men, took the raft in tow, and vanished into the night.

Inside the cove Doc had found freshly sawed cookies, and the pattern of Jarvis' strategy had become plain. Unknown to Doc, Jarvis had dropped the skiff and men while still some distance from the cove, then had cruised along the island until Doc had discovered him. After that, Jarvis had merely kept Doc interested while the men in the skiff had taken as many logs as they could handle, sawed off the brand and restamped them, then put out to sea to be picked up by the tug. It had been an amazing simple yet clever trick.

"I was mousetrapped," Doc concluded.

"Mousetrapped?" Gramps was puzzled.

"It's a trick football play," Tim explained. Chuck stifled a chuckle. Tim had already declared that he wasn't interested in football, yet he had indicated that he understood at least one technical point of the game.

Gramps stirred uneasily in his chair. "Doc wasn't at fault," Tim went on loyally. "I'd have done the same if I had been in his place. I've already told him that Jarvis would have stolen the logs anyway. Isn't that right, Gramps?"

"Of course," the old man replied readily. "I've lived long enough not to be surprised at hard luck." He slid his hands up and down the rifle barrel. "Too bad, though, I wasn't there, with this gun!" he added grimly. "But we're forced to keep it a one-sided fight. Maybe Jarvis will show up here at the cabin some day. If he does, I'll be ready for him! Meanwhile, I don't figure to let you youngsters try fightin' him with his own weapons. Rather lose every stick on the island than let anything happen to you. Anyway, he ain't licked us yet. We'll keep tryin'!"

"I have a plan," Doc ventured. "At the moment it's no more than an idea, and maybe it won't work. No use talking about it until I'm certain."

"Go ahead, boy." Gramps sounded discouraged. It was evident that he didn't think much of Doc's plan, whatever it might be. Chuck guessed that Tim probably felt the same way. But they didn't know Doc as well as he did. If Doc had what he called a plan, then it was well worth considering. He was unusually studious for a boy whose first love seemed to be athletics; he read books which would have bored Chuck to impatience. Already he had picked up a surprising amount of information about forestry matters that many a college undergraduate probably didn't know. His explanation was that the more he knew about such things, the easier it would be for him when he entered forestry school.

Even Lem Jarvis might be astonished before Doc was finished. It seemed hard to believe that the log pirate could be outwitted, yet Chuck had vast respect for Doc's ability to think fast and straight.

Yet Doc, although confessing to a pardonable mistake, was still determined to show how badly he felt about it. He told Tim, "You must be tired after rowing that skiff twenty miles. The least I can do is take over your patrol tonight, so you can get some rest. I'll feel better if I do."

But Tim shook his head. "Thanks, Doc," he said,

81

"but I don't think it will be necessary to do any more patrolling tonight. It will take Jarvis a long while to tow those logs to some mill on the mainland, and my guess is that when he's done the job, he'll want rest as much as we do. We won't need to worry about him for a day or so, although we'll start the patrol again tomorrow night. He won't show up during daylight. Isn't that the way you figure it, Gramps?"

The old man nodded. "I'd bet on it," he declared. "No use of you boys gettin' tuckered out until you have to!"

"About time we had something to eat," said Tim. Nobody disagreed with him. The hour was late, and so many exciting things had happened since morning that somehow the matter of eating had been sidetracked.

Tim went to work. He was obviously experienced at cooking, inasmuch as he had been doing it for his grandfather and himself for a long while. In no time he had a smoking dinner on the table in the little kitchen off the main living room, but not until he had carried a tray to Gramps did he sit down with Chuck and Doc.

They took charge of washing the dishes for him, and after that he showed them a side room where they could spread their sleeping bags. Then he helped Gramps to bed, an arm around the old man's shoulders. Soon quiet settled over the cabin.

It seemed to Chuck that he had scarcely closed his eyes when he opened them, blinking in the strong sunlight which flooded the room.

Doc was still sleeping. Chuck dressed and went out to the living room, thinking that he could at least start a fire to have the place warmed when Gramps arose. But he saw that the old man was already in his accustomed place at the window, looking up the hillside as if he hoped to see Lem Jarvis sneaking up on the cabin. Tim and Kamooks were not in sight.

"We get up early on Skookum-Chuck," Gramps explained. "Tim and the dog went over the hill for a look at the logs in the cove. Ought to be back before long."

In the harsh morning light Gramps appeared older, more tired, and it seemed to Chuck that fresh lines of worry were etched deeply into the seamed face. The reason for it wasn't hard to understand. Another batch of logs had been stolen. More of Tim's hard work had gone for naught. The Elliotts on Skookum-Chuck Island had been fighting a losing battle whose end—total defeat—seemed not far off. Probably Gramps had not slept well. Yet now he tried to force cheerfulness and confidence into his manner.

"Tim aims to start loggin' again today," he announced. He smiled. "We hope to cut 'em faster than Jarvis can steal 'em! You boys know anything about knockin' down trees?"

Chuck shook his head. "I've seen it done," he replied, "but I've never tried it myself. I don't think Doc has, either. But we can learn."

"High time you did," Gramps told him. "Bull Harmon knew all there was to know about the loggin' game, and I reckon he'd want his grandson to be the same way."

83

The door opened; Tim stood there, Kamooks behind him. Tim nodded to Chuck, then told Gramps seriously, "Jarvis made a good job of it this time. Got some of our best logs, sticks that would have brought us nearly a hundred dollars apiece!"

Gramps wagged his head, his face grim. "I'm not surprised! Jarvis knows good timber." Then his voice became harsh. "All I want is to live long enough to make him pay for what he's done! Even if I have to drag myself out of this chair and settle his hash with a gun!" He sat upright, face flushed, and it seemed to Chuck for a moment that the old man was angry enough to get up and force his useless legs to carry him across the floor.

Tim went to his side quickly and said, "Don't get excited, Gramps. We'll lick Jarvis, put him behind bars, where he belongs, but we won't shoot him."

He patted the old man's shoulder. "As soon as I can rustle breakfast, we're going to do some logging. Maybe with the help of Chuck and Doc," he added hopefully, "I could build a wooden breakwater across the mouth of the lagoon, so that we could keep the logs here instead of at the cove."

Gramps shook his head. "You know better than that, Tim," he said querulously. "No breakwater like that would hold. First storm that came along would scatter our timber all over Puget Sound, and then Jarvis and other log pirates would really have a harvest! Only safe place on Skookum-Chuck is where we've been keepin' 'em—in the cove."

"Why not build another cabin there, and move

over to the cove so that the logs could be watched day and night?" Chuck asked. It seemed like a simple solution of the problem, so simple, indeed, that he knew there must be a catch in it.

"No fresh water at the cove," Tim explained. "The only spring on the island is here."

Doc appeared, yawning. "Best sleep I've had in months," he declared. He looked hungry. "Breakfast ready?"

Tim grinned. "Coming up," he replied. It seemed to Chuck that Tim was more relaxed than when they had first met him, even though he had just been robbed of another batch of logs. Probably Tim had been lonely, and he was beginning to enjoy the company of two boys his own age.

It was a good breakfast he prepared, and it didn't take him long to get it ready. When he had placed the food on the table, and again carried a tray of it to Gramps before touching any himself, he told them, "Eat hearty! We're going to knock down some timber today."

Doc, however, did not appear enthusiastic at the prospect. "Do you mind," he asked Tim, "if I tackle a job of my own, instead? I did some thinking before I fell asleep last night, and maybe I've got the problem solved."

Chuck's tone was humorous. "Another Play Twenty-Two?"

"Call it that," Doc said shortly. "All right with you, Tim?"

"Sure," the latter told him. "Chuck and I can

handle this logging job. But why not let us in on the big secret?"

"Not yet," Doc answered. "If it doesn't work after all, Chuck would never let me forget it. I've got to be sure." He added, "I'll need a blowtorch. If you tell me you have one, then I'll know I'm really in luck."

Tim seemed surprised. "It so happens that we do have one," he said. "Before Gramps was hurt he brought one from the mainland. He used it to take some of the temper out of a falling-saw whose teeth were so hard that they couldn't be sharpened with a file. What on earth do you want it for?"

Chuck smiled. "Tim," he reminded the other, "when you get to playing football, you'll learn not to ask questions of the quarterback. Let Mr. Genius, here, call the plays in his own way!"

"Hah!" Doc bared his teeth at Chuck, although his eyes were twinkling. "Never saw a team yet that didn't need *somebody* to do its thinking! Who was it planned most of your touchdowns, Mr. Muscles?" Tim laughed. This was the sort of thing he'd been missing, and he loved every bit of it.

They washed the dishes, cleaned up the cabin, and Tim found the blowtorch for Doc. Then Tim led Chuck up the hillside to the scene of the hand-logging operation.

Kamooks wanted to go along, but at a word from Tim the wolf-dog settled down in the living room with Gramps. Kamooks' limp had nearly disappeared. His wound was healing rapidly, and soon he'd be ready to do whatever he could in maintaining the Skookum-Chuck patrol. In his own way he was as useful as any of them; at least, Chuck thought with a touch of chagrin, Kamooks had prevented *one* attempt to steal logs, which was more than his human allies had done.

The two boys carried tools which Tim said they would need—a falling-saw, a pair of double-bitted axes, and a coil of light but strong twisted-steel cable which had a metal hook secured to one end of it by means of a clevis and pin which could be removed easily when necessary. Tim explained that he used the cable as a "choker" in moving a tree after it had been cut down. Such other gear as they would use was already cached up there on the hillside, but the axes and saw were always kept in a toolshed at the cabin to protect them against rusting.

"Ever swing an ax?" Tim asked.

"Some," Chuck admitted. On visits he and Doc had made to woods camps of the Sound Logging Company, they had watched expert loggers at work, and had even tried using axes themselves. They had found that it required considerable skill to drive a keen, double-edged blade time after time into the same exact cut, but Chuck had thought that he had become rather good at it. But under the critical eyes of Tim, who had been using an ax ever since he was big enough to lift one, it seemed wise for Chuck to act modest.

They reached the place at last. Here was evidence that Tim had put in many long hours of hard work taking logs off the hillside. From the top of the ridge down to the sea was a bare streak some two hundred yards wide where only stumps and piles of brush and hacked-off limbs remained. The ground was scored with shallow trenches where stick after stick had plunged wildly down the slope toward salt water.

At this altitude Chuck could enjoy a remarkable panoramic view of the San Juans. The wind had driven every trace of fog out of the air; the morning sky was a soft blue, and the breeze-stroked water shimmered under the summer sun like vast acres of glittering diamonds. All about, scores of islands, some large, some small, were scattered, most of them thickly wooded, like Skookum-Chuck, although a few were bleak and high-banked. Along the watery channels moved toy-like craft of different sizes, pleasure-craft, commercial fishermen, a few tugs towing log-rafts. To the eastward the unbroken coast of the mainland was marked here and there by smoke rising from sawmills.

Tim also stood quiet, looking around, as though he, too, enjoyed the sight. Then he touched Chuck's arm, and pointed. "See that big and fast tug, coming out from the mainland?" he asked.

Chuck nodded. The craft, he guessed, must be two or three miles away, yet in the clear air its outlines were plainly visible. It was too big to be the one which Lem Jarvis owned. That it had abundant speed and power was indicated by the frothing bow wave which split from each side of its prow.

"That's one of the regular log patrol tugs," Tim

88

explained. "They're out on a scouting trip after that wind we had last night. Rafts get broken up and the logs scattered. The patrol tugs make sure that Jarvis or some other log pirate doesn't pick up loose sticks."

After a moment he added, a touch of bitterness in his voice, "They're looking for timber belonging to the Sound Logging Company, or some other big outfit. That tug won't come near Skookum-Chuck. Gramps and I can't afford to pay for that kind of protection!"

Chuck made no reply, and after a moment Tim said in a changed voice, "Guess I shouldn't talk that way. The boys in the log patrol can't afford to work for nothing. It costs plenty to operate a fleet of big tugs like that. They'd help us in a second if we could trap Jarvis—they don't like log pirates any better than we do. But it isn't reasonable to expect them to look after our logs unless they get paid for it."

"You mentioned the regular log patrol several times," Chuck remarked. "I still don't understand how it works, or why it can't give you protection."

"Simple enough," Tim replied. "The patrol is a private company, chartered by the state and given authority to pick up any loose logs found floating in Puget Sound. When loose logs are found, a patrol tug takes them to the booming grounds, where a log-scaler figures the number of board feet in each stick. The owner of the log has to pay towing and other charges as well as a percentage of what the stick is actually worth before he can recover it. The patrol is the only outfit which has authority to pick up loose logs; if a stick, whether it is branded or not, is found in the possession of somebody who isn't the real owner, then he is supposed by the authorities to be trying to steal it. That's grand larceny, and the penalty for it is heavy."

"But," Chuck persisted, "I should think that even if the log patrol did pick up one of your loose sticks, you'd get *some* money back, even after you paid those towing and other charges."

"Sure we would," Tim agreed, "but we can't afford to lose most of what the log is really worth. We'd rather take a chance on recovering our own timber if it gets away, as sometimes happens. So we have an understanding with the log patrol that they are not to bother with our logs. In that way we win everything, or else lose everything! Gramps figures that in the long run, we're money ahead.

"Jarvis knows the log patrol isn't interested in our timber," Tim went on. "That's why he isn't afraid to grab one of our logs wherever he can find one, and even raid our raft in the cove.

"Most of the other hand-loggers like Gramps and myself are so poor that they have to take the same chances as we do. Jarvis steals their logs just as he steals ours."

Tim sighed. "Sometimes," he declared gloomily, "I think that even Gramps feels like giving up!"

"But he won't!" said Chuck positively. "And neither will you, Tim. I don't think either of you is that sort."

90

"I've never felt we were quitters," Tim asserted. "Well," and he looked about, "let's get to work!"

He indicated a fir nearly four feet thick at the butt. "We'll take that one," he decided. "Grab hold of one end of this saw. We'll cut a notch."

Chuck obeyed, although well aware that he wasn't familiar with the use of a crosscut saw, but he reasoned that if he kept quiet and did as he was told, and at the same time watched Tim, he might pick up some fine points about logging.

The notch, he observed, was to be cut into the down-hill face of the tree. The reason for this was plain; the tree would fall with its top pointed down the slope, and later could be sent sliding toward salt water without offering the resistance of its wide, square-cut base.

Tim started the notch about three feet above ground, just at the point where the trunk flared downward to join with its roots. The sharp teeth of the saw sang musically as they began eating through bark and green wood. Chuck, wanting to help all he could, pulled and pushed the saw at top strength until Tim shook his head disapprovingly.

"Take it easy," the Skookum-Chuck boy advised. "You'll be tired out in ten minutes at that rate. Besides, you'll tire *me,* as well!"

He added, "Don't push the saw at all, but let me pull it toward myself. Then you pull it back on the next stroke. Don't bear down so hard, either. Let the saw do the work!"

Chuck obeyed, and suddenly found the effort much

easier. The saw actually seemed to cooperate, for its tone became rythmical and business-like. He wasn't working half so hard, yet the blade was biting steadily into the tree.

They kept at it until the cut was about a foot deep, or one-quarter the diameter of the tree. Then Tim pulled out the saw and laid it aside. "Got to chop out the notch," he explained. "Let's see if you can use an ax."

Tim picked up an ax, swung it smoothly, and the blade sank into bark and wood. "As soon as I've taken a stroke and lifted my ax," he told Chuck, "you take a stroke yourself. In that way we'll keep clear of each other."

Chuck tried it, but with small success at first. He had strength enough to drive the blade deeply into the tree, but he lacked accuracy. Tim, however, made every stroke count. Big chips leaped away from the tree trunk. Manfully, Chuck kept at it, and soon his aim became better. It wasn't long before an angular notch had been chopped just above where the saw-cut had been made. Then Tim called a halt.

Shoving the head of his double-bitted ax into the notch, he squinted along the wooden handle, which pointed in a downhill direction. "If we've cut the notch evenly," he told Chuck, "the ax handle will show just where the tree is going to fall. It's an old logger's trick."

Apparently he was satisfied with what the ax handle indicated, for he said, "Now we'll put in the back-cut."

This time they began sawing on the opposite side of the tree, some two inches above the bottom of the notch. It was important, Tim explained, to keep the saw exactly parallel to the other cut, so that the tree would fall straight when the time came for it to go down, rather than swing aside. Now and then Tim asked Chuck how many inches of solid wood remained, and thereafter he moved the saw sideways to make the necessary correction.

It was apparent to him why the falling-saw had such a narrow blade, for this enabled Tim to drive a thin wedge into the cut when the wood began to tighten. Not only did this permit the saw to run more freely, but it likewise permitted him to force the tree to fall in the direction he wished it to go.

At last Chuck saw that only about two inches of solid wood remained between the back-cut and the notch. The saw was pulled out, and Tim picked up the maul again, telling Chuck, "Stand clear and get ready to run. Sometimes a tree jumps off the stump and lashes out behind in any direction." As Chuck backed away, Tim began pounding the wedge deeper into the cut.

The top of the tree began slanting slowly in a downhill direction. Twice more the maul drove the wedge deeper, actually tipping the trunk off the stump. Now the trunk leaned alarmingly; there were ominous, cracking sounds as the wood between the back-cut and the notch broke suddenly. Tim dropped the maul and ran to join Chuck well up on the hillside. There was a whispering sigh from the widespread limbs as the trunk swished through the air, faster and faster, and then the tree fell, with a thud which made the ground quake.

The tree was tipped so sharply down the slope that it would have started sliding had not the limbs acted as a brake. Tim next picked up the "choker," using the hook to take a single turn of the cable around the butt of the tree. The other end was wound several times around the solid stump, and drawn tight, and the tree was anchored. "Now," he announced, "we'll take off the limbs. Don't want the stick to get away from us until we're ready."

Chuck picked up an ax, as did Tim, and the boys went to work. When the last limb had been hacked off, they had a tapering pole or stick some hundred and twenty-five feet long. The top, or end lowest down the hill, was cut off and sharpened to a spear-like point, Tim explaining that it would offer little resistance to ground over which it would pass, or brush which might be in its way.

"Got a bucket of grease over there," and he indicated an old windfall nearby. "Usually I smear some of it on the lower end of a stick. But I think this stick is going to slide down without any help."

He picked up the maul again, and began tapping the pin which held the clevis and hook to the cable, standing away from it as far as possible. Chuck felt like holding his breath as Tim worked. The cable was going to let go suddenly, and it was not hard to see that the loosened end might whip around viciously, for the weight of the big stick aimed downhill had drawn the wire as taut as a violin string. Yet Tim appeared to understand the danger, too, and he worked cautiously, ready to leap backward at the critical moment.

The light tapping went on; then there was a sharp, pinging noise, and the cable fell free. A fraction of a second later the stick made a slithering sound, and started downward, gathering momentum swiftly.

Charging ahead, twisting its long length over the uneven ground, the stick speeded up, its progress downward a succession of thunderous bumps, and a few moments later it shot clear of the hillside and dived into the water with a tremendous splash.

Tim stared downward as the stick buried almost its entire length in the sea, striking the water at a flat angle, then quickly reappearing. Chuck was so awed by what he had seen that he could think of nothing to say.

But Tim's voice was matter-of-fact. "Got to get a bucking-saw from the cabin," he announced. "That stick has to be cut into log lengths. Then we'll make a raft and anchor it so that the tide won't carry the logs away." He led the way toward the cabin.

Doc was nowhere in sight, but Gramps as usual was sitting by his window. His eyes glowed with pride as he saw Tim.

"Heard you take down another tree," he remarked. "Seems like you made short work of it." He grinned at Chuck. "How do you like the way Bull Harmon used to make his livin'?"

Chuck shook his head. "He must have been a better

man than I'll ever hope to be," he declared. "I felt pretty useless."

"Don't you believe it, Gramps," Tim declared. "Chuck will be a full-fledged logger within a few weeks. He learns fast."

"Born in him, I reckon," Gramps commented. He looked around. "Doc is off by himself, some place. Said to tell you boys he's goin' to be busy all mornin', and doesn't want to be bothered. You reckon that lad really has somethin' on his mind?"

"I'll bet on it!" Chuck said warmly.

"Got me puzzled," Gramps said. "He's been askin' me a lot of questions about the length of logs. Told him we usually cut 'em thirty-two feet long, but sometimes they run only twenty-eight feet, or maybe thirty. He wanted to know if a mill owner was likely to be suspicious of a short log, figurin' that it might have been stolen and the branded ends sawed off. Told him it didn't matter much, unless a man's logs were *always* under thirty-two feet. That seemed to make him excited."

Chuck smiled. "Doc surely is on the trail of another Play Twenty-Two!" he declared. "It will be something to watch if it turns out the way he expects it."

Gramps made an odd sound deep in his throat. "Football!" he exclaimed. "Pretty soon I'll be talkin' the same lingo." He stirred in his chair and told Tim, "Best get that stick bucked up before the tide carries it away." Then he resumed his staring out of the window.

"We're on our way, Gramps," Tim replied. "If Chuck and I can knock down another tree and buck it up before dark, we'll have a new batch of high-grade logs. That will make up for the logs Jarvis stole yesterday."

Cutting the stick into proper lengths, Chuck found, wasn't nearly as complicated and dangerous as the actual falling of the tree had been. He was able to help Tim, although the latter insisted the real work was a one-man job which he could best do alone.

With the skiff, they towed the stick to the float, and Chuck held it in place there while Tim marked off the log-lengths, then drove his bucking-saw, heavier and wider-bladed than the one they had used to drop the tree, up and down in the water at a steep angle. When the job was done they had three good logs a full thirty-two feet in length, as well as a smaller stick which came from the treetop and was fit only for firewood, Tim explained. By means of heavy spikes driven into each log, and a few lengths of rope, a small raft was made up and secured alongside the float until more trees could be cut.

Walking the logs as the raft was made up was a task which Chuck left to Tim, for the latter's steel-calked boots gave him sure-footedness. Chuck's own rubber-soled shoes did not provide the same solid traction. At each step Tim took, he left a pattern of tiny holes in the rough bark.

Suddenly Chuck gave an exclamation. "I've got it!" he cried. "I know a way by which you can identify your logs after they're stolen!"

Tim swung around, an awed look on his face. Then he smiled. "Mean to say," he asked banteringly, "that we have *two* geniuses on Skookum-Chuck?"

"I know it is going to sound simple," Chuck replied stubbornly. "Maybe it's too simple to work. But it's worth trying." He squatted down on the float, beside the raft, and his right forefinger began tracing out the rows of marks left by the metal calks.

7 ... Baiting the Trap

*C*huck looked at Tim and asked, "Is it easy to change the way those calks are set in your soles?"

"Sure," Tim replied. He reached into his trousers pocket and pulled out a tiny socket wrench. "I carry this with me all the time," he explained. "Also, a few extra calks. Then, if a calk tears loose, I use this wrench to replace it." He sat down on the float, slipped the little wrench over one of the steel points, and quickly unscrewed it from the leather. "Like that."

Chuck nodded. "Thought so! Now," he went on, "supposing that you removed the calks from the center of each sole, then reset them until they formed the letters of your brand, HE. Every time you walked the length of a log, you'd be putting your brand on the bark, wouldn't you?"

Tim's eyes widened in understanding, even admiration. "Sure!" he agreed. "Probably Jarvis would never notice those marks, either. He'd only be interested in cutting the brand off the *end* of the logs. And unless he peeled off all the bark as well, we could still prove that they were our logs!"

"It's worth a try," Chuck declared. "But how would you know where to find your logs after they were stolen?"

Tim gestured toward the mainland. "I could search the log pond of every mill over there," he said. "I don't know where Jarvis is selling the timber—maybe to several different mills—but sooner or later we'd find the right one.

"I don't think those mill-owners even suspect that the logs are stolen. They probably believe that Jarvis has an operation of his own somewhere among these islands, or that maybe he buys from hand-loggers. The mill owners will work with us, I'm sure. If we spoil Jarvis' market, maybe he'll leave our sticks alone!"

Chuck laughed. "Let's not tell Doc about this," he suggested. "Let's keep it as a surprise. I'd like to show Mr. Genius that *we* can figure out a Play Twenty-Two as well as he can!"

Tim likewise laughed. They shook hands on it. Of a sudden the situation, seemingly so hopeless, had brightened immensely.

Tim set about changing his calks. "Just so that every log I walk on hereafter carries the HE brand," he explained. "I'll take the first patrol tonight, and I'll walk the length of every log in the cove. Then, if

Jarvis manages to steal any more timber while we're not looking, we'll have him trapped!"

He began striding back and forth on the rafted logs. The imprint of the letters HE showed sharp and clear. "Too clear," he decided finally. "Jarvis isn't blind. It will be odd if he doesn't notice those marks. But we'll have to take that chance."

Thereafter, they went back up the hillside and began cutting another stick of timber. When quitting time came they had six fine logs rafted beside the float. Chuck was weary, yet he felt the glow of achievement; he had made a good start toward becoming a skilled logger, as his grandfather, Bull Harmon, had been.

Doc seemed mysterious, and had little to say. "How's the big idea working out?" Chuck asked. He was jubilant over the plan he and Tim had hit upon.

"It works," Doc replied shortly. "All I need now is to plan the next move!"

"How?"

"You'll know," Doc evaded, "in good time!"

Chuck winked at Tim. "Maybe," he remarked, "we won't need Doc's big idea after all. We've been doing a little planning ourselves. Right, Tim?"

Tim nodded importantly. Doc looked surprised, yet his voice was incredulous. "You'll have to prove it," he asserted. "This," he added loftily, "is a job for an expert, not amateurs!"

Gramps chuckled. "Don't know what you youngsters are talkin' about," he remarked, "but it lifts my hope, somehow. I'd bet that Lem Jarvis is in for the biggest surprise of his life!" Gramps' cheerfulness sounded real, and it was good to hear, Chuck thought.

That night the patrol was resumed, with Tim taking the first watch, Chuck the next, and Doc the last. But there was no activity on the part of Jarvis. Perhaps he suspected that a trap of some sort had been set, and he had decided to be careful. Doc, when he returned to the lagoon soon after daylight, brought two or more of the wooden cookies, saying that he wished to continue his experiments.

Chuck and Tim were agreeable, as they had work of their own to do. Their job was to use the power skiff to tow the new raft to the cove. A half-dozen logs were about all that the craft could handle at one time. They waited until the tide had turned and was flowing in the direction of the cove, then the sturdy little motor pulled the raft along at good speed. To Tim it must have seemed a luxury, for he had been compelled to tow the logs with no other power than his arms and a pair of oars, and the job usually took at least four times as long. Soon the new logs, not only carrying the usual brand at their ends, but with the HE pattern stamped on the bark, were joined with the other sticks behind the boom. Then the next move was up to Jarvis.

Maybe the tug from the sawmill would call at the cove in time to remove the logs before the pirates came; maybe it would be delayed, which often happened, Tim explained, thus giving Jarvis opportunity for another raid.

They went back home, and resumed logging. By nightfall another raft of new sticks had been moored to the float. But because the hour was late, Tim decided to wait until the following day before taking them to the cove. Also, the tide wasn't favorable.

Yet when the evening meal was finished, they came out of the cabin to discover that a change in the weather had taken place. A southwest wind had sprung up, and there was the smell of coming rain in the air. Waves were already beginning to pound into the lagoon.

"Tim," Gramps remarked, worry in his voice, "you should have taken those logs to the cove, no matter if it is dark and the tide is wrong. Too late now, I reckon. There's a good chance that we'll lose those sticks, if the wind gets stronger before mornin'."

"I can see that," Tim agreed soberly. There were another six logs in the new raft, and when sold to the mill they would bring considerable money to the Elliotts. It was no wonder, Chuck thought, that Gramps was uneasy.

Twice Tim went down to the float to make sure that

the logs were secure. The second time he returned he wagged his head gloomily.

"Gramps is right," he announced. "We're in for trouble. The tide and the waves have set up a bad crosscurrent, and the raft will probably break apart. The ropes won't hold much longer, and I've even tried using wire cable, but the spikes keep pulling out of the logs. By morning those sticks will probably be scattered everywhere."

"Got any ideas?" Chuck asked.

"We'll have to use the motor skiff to haul them back one by one when they break loose," Tim replied. "But that means we can't use the same boat to guard the logs in the cove. This may be the time that Jarvis decides to help himself to them."

"One of us could take the trail over the hill to the cove," Chuck suggested, "and stand guard on shore there. That would leave two of us to keep these logs from getting away."

Tim nodded. "That's the way we'll do it," he declared. "I'd better stay here, because I know more about handling those sticks. Who wants to help me?"

"I'll tackle it," Doc offered. "I feel as though I've been dodging work lately. I'd like to make it up."

"Think you can guard the logs in the cove?" Tim asked Chuck.

"I'll try, of course," the latter replied. "Kamooks could help me. At least he'll be good company."

Tim nodded approval. "Kamooks will also keep you on the trail over the hill," he told Chuck. "Well, let's get started!"

Gramps said mournfully, "Wish I could help, instead of sittin' here and twiddlin' my thumbs! Doesn't seem fair, somehow. But maybe someday," he added wrathfully, "I'll get Lem Jarvis lined up in the sights of this old gun. *Then* I can be a lot of help!"

"Easy, Gramps!" Tim cautioned. "We've agreed to do this job without any shooting."

"Maybe we did," the old man admitted aggrievedly, "but I reckon I can always change my mind, can't I? In the old days, loggers would have taken a man like Jarvis and strung him up from a limb of the nearest tree!"

Tim smiled tolerantly. "But the old days have gone, Gramps," he reminded the other. He turned to Kamooks, gave the dog a swift pat on the head. "You're all healed up and as good as ever," he told the big dog. "You go with Chuck—and take good care of him!"

Kamooks whined and wagged his tail. Maybe he didn't understand fully what Tim had said, and yet somehow he seemed to know that there was a task ahead, perhaps danger and excitement. Chuck opened the door and said, "Okay, Kamooks!" and the dog followed him willingly.

Darkness had come, and the wind moaned among the trees along the trail. From the direction of the lagoon came the steady crash of waves, and when Chuck was halfway up the slope, he looked back and saw a light bobbing where the float must be. Tim and Doc had a lantern, and were already busy in an effort

107

to keep the logs from escaping. He turned and went on, aware that he had a job of his own to do.

Kamooks had taken the lead from the beginning, as though he knew well where they were going. This suited Chuck, for among the thickly growing trees the darkness was so intense that he could hardly make out the trail. Yet Kamooks knew where it was, and all Chuck had to do was to keep close behind the dog.

The breeze increased, and by the time the top of the ridge was reached, it was threatening to become a gale. Tim and Doc would surely be busy! Yet the wind was not cold, and there was no rain. Chuck and Kamooks went down the slope, and once the cove was reached, there was hardly any breeze; the high ridge behind it served as an effective windbreak. It was easy to see why the Elliotts had chosen this cove as a moorage for their logs, instead of the exposed lagoon.

Soon they were at the camp where the first night had been spent. It seemed as good a place as any to stay while maintaining watch. Chuck put one of the wooden disks flat on the ground, and braced another upright behind it as a backrest. Kamooks settled down beside him on the sand. It was going to be a long, tiresome vigil.

The log-raft, held in place by boomsticks, was no more than a dark line on the lighter-colored water. One end of the raft, he noted, was close to the beach, for the tide was going out and the water was lowering in the cove. It didn't seem probable that Jarvis would show up. He was probably elsewhere tonight, maybe staying in port because of the wind. And yet the very fact that he had not bothered the logs in the cove for several days might be a hint that he was ready to strike again. Chuck had no definite plan if the pirates should come; he'd have to wait and see and determine his strategy when the time came. The best he could hope for, it seemed, was that he could scare them away. Once let them know that the logs were being guarded, and they might give up. After all, it was a big risk Jarvis and his men were taking. If something went wrong, and they were caught, it could mean long prison sentences for them. Saw logs were valuable, and they had already stolen hundreds of dollars' worth of them from the Elliotts, maybe thousands of dollars'.

The darkness deepened, and even the indistinct line of the log-raft faded out at last. There was a heavy overcast which blotted out the stars. He could hear the crying of the wind on the ridge back of him, but down here the air was comparatively still.

Time passed. Boredom took hold of him. It would have been far more exciting, he decided, to have helped Tim and Doc round up logs drifting away from the lagoon. Still, the job he was doing was important, too, even though it was terribly monotonous.

He yawned. He had worked hard and long that day, and at the moment he could think of nothing more wonderful than being able to crawl into his sleeping bag back at the cabin, instead of sitting here on a hard, flat disk of wood, and staring unseeingly into the night. Yet he mustn't fall asleep. Tim and the others were depending on him; he mustn't let them down. But the yawning became more persistent. He changed position, settling himself more comfortably, leaning back and relaxing. His eyelids felt so heavy that he could not resist closing them for a moment . . .

Then they flew open abruptly, and he sat up, startled, for Kamooks had growled, softly yet warningly.

Chuck listened. He was no longer tired, and he sensed that he had been really asleep—for a long while. The sound of the wind in the trees back on the ridge had died away; the night had fallen silent, ominously so, it seemed to him.

Kamooks growled again. Then Chuck heard a new sound—the far-off thump of a diesel engine. It could mean much, or nothing. It might come from Jarvis' tug, but it also could have been made by the engine of an honest craft which had been caught by night and the recent wind far from its home port. Then came a new noise, steady and yet cautious, and his pulse quickened in sudden alarm. It was the creak of oarlocks; there could be no mistake, for he had heard the same sound previously, when Jarvis' men had attempted to raid the cove during the fog. The pirate tug was somewhere out there in the blackness, its engine idling, while its skiff was heading toward shore.

Chuck stood up, and Kamooks rose also, as though awaiting orders. It was hard for Chuck to decide what to do. If he merely yelled, to let the men know that their stealthy approach had been discovered, they might turn back in a hurry—or they might not! The tug itself might attempt to dash into the cove, to put a towline on the log-raft and escape to sea before anybody could stop them. Still, the tide must have fully ebbed by now, in which case the entrance to the little harbor might be too shallow for Jarvis to risk grounding his craft.

While he pondered the situation, the sound of the oarlocks became more distinct. The skiff had passed through the entrance; it was no more than a hundred yards distant from him now. A few moments later he heard it bump gently against the boomsticks of the raft. Then came metallic clinks as tools were lifted out. He heard the men talking in low tones as they moved away from the skiff and out upon the raft.

And suddenly he had a daring notion! It was an idea which seemed wild and risky, yet the unexpectedness of it might bring success.

He was going to steal the skiff! If he did that, took it out of the cove and at the same time managed to keep away from the tug by staying close to shore, the men would be trapped on the island. Then, with the help of Tim and Doc—perhaps using Gramps' rifle as a threatening persuader—the men might be captured.

It was possible, of course, that they were armed, but he guessed that would be unlikely. They weren't looking for a fight; they didn't expect even to meet opposition. Besides, a load of such tools as a saw, pike poles, a maul, and such other things as they would need, would overload the skiff which carried at least two men.

He whispered to Kamooks, standing beside him, "Careful, boy!" The big dog started to whine in suppressed excitement, but a touch of Chuck's hand stopped him. Then the two of them moved quietly down the beach to where Chuck knew some of the logs lay close to shore.

Out there in the darkness he could hear the men working. By now, he reasoned, they must believe that the cove was unguarded. Feeling the way with his feet, careful not to take a misstep, he reached the logs and began walking over them toward the spot where, he judged, the skiff was moored alongside them.

Farther down the raft the men sounded as though they were loosening the wire cable which joined the ends of the boomsticks. He was sure they hadn't heard him. Kamooks followed, as noiseless as a ghost.

At last Chuck saw the shadow of the skiff just in front of him. He groped along its rail until he came to the rope securing it to the boomsticks. But he found the rope drawn so tightly that he could not unfasten it, and to get the slack he needed, he pulled on the end tied inside the skiff. As he did so he heard a clanking noise, and instantly knew that a loop of the line had caught hold of some tool left behind in the boat.

There was sudden silence on the part of the men, and he knew that he had been heard. Then came their excited voices, and he heard them coming toward him. He'd have to act fast! He managed to untie the rope from the boomsticks and, guessing where a seat or thwart of the skiff must be, jumped into the craft.

Yet he misjudged the distance. Instead of a thwart he stepped on the gunwale; the skiff tipped sharply, and the next moment he had plunged into the water.

He went under, but came up swimming, his immediate effort being to get as far away from the skiff as possible before the men arrived. He heard their feet pounding across the logs. Evidently they had no lantern with them. One of them yelled, "Hook that boat with your pike pole!" The skiff must have shifted away from the boomsticks. There were clattering sounds as the steel-pointed pole struck the rail of the boat several times. Then came a loud splash.

"What's that?" one of them demanded.

"Who knows?" retorted the other. "Let's get out of here!"

Stroking swiftly, careful not to splash, Chuck pulled away in the darkness. Then he was aware that he was not alone; there was another swimmer beside him. His hand reached out and touched fur. That second splash had been made by Kamooks!

The wolf-dog had quickly made a choice. Probably his first impulse had been to give battle to the men on the raft, yet Chuck might need help. Kamooks had gone into the water and overtaken the boy whom he regarded as his friend.

Chuck was a good swimmer, yet the water was bitterly cold, and he was hampered by his shoes and clothing. The men might hear him, decide to run him down and finish him. The thing to do was to get as far away as he could, and as quickly as possible. He grabbed hold of Kamooks' neck fur with his left hand, while he stroked with his right. The dog, a powerful swimmer, seemed to understand. Together they moved rapidly toward shore.

Yet there was no pursuit; apparently Jarvis' men, taken by surprise, wanted only to get away. They didn't understand the true situation; for all they knew a trap was closing on them. Guessing at their panic, Chuck half raised himself from the water and yelled loudly, "Tim! Doc! Head 'em off at the entrance!"

It was a bluff, of course, but it seemed to work well. He heard the rapid splashing of their oars as they pulled frantically for the mouth of the cove. Minutes later, when Chuck and the dog reached shore, he still heard the diminishing beat of their oars. There was a bumping sound as the skiff came alongside the tug. More excited talk. Then the throb of the idling diesel quickened, and he knew that the tug was heading outward.

For a long moment he and the dog stood there on the beach, water dripping from them. The beating of the tug's engine became fainter. Chuck felt jubilant at the way things had turned out. He'd outwitted Jarvis again!

Yet common sense told him that he needn't expect to come up with a fresh trick next time. Jarvis was crafty. And he wouldn't give up as long as he had opportunity to steal several hundred dollars' worth of logs without much risk of being caught.

Chuck guessed that Jarvis wouldn't be back again tonight; dawn could not be far off. He shivered in his drenched clothes. All he wanted at the moment was to get back to the cabin and crawl into his sleeping bag.

Besides, he was anxious to learn how luck had treated Tim and Doc. Both of them would have had to work hard to save the logs in the lagoon. For all Chuck knew otherwise, all the trouble he and Tim had taken to harvest those logs had been wasted.

With mixed feelings he and Kamooks started off on the trail for home.

8 ... Disappointment

There was a light in the cabin as Chuck and Kamooks came down the trail. When Chuck opened the door at last, he found Gramps in the latter's accustomed place at the window, while Doc was helping Tim prepare breakfast. All of them seemed sober, preoccupied. They looked at him wonderingly as he entered, wet clothes clinging dankly to him. Kamooks lay down in front of the open fire, and began licking his damp fur.

Yet they asked no questions, and Chuck went to his pack and got into a change of dry clothing before he told them what had happened at the cove. Gramps said grimly, "You took a big chance, boy! But your plan might have worked. Kamooks could have tracked down that pair if they'd been trapped on the island. Reckon Jarvis would have had a fit, but there wouldn't have been much he could have done about it." His hand gripped the gun barrel firmly. "I'd have guaranteed that they'd have talked—plenty!"

116

He added in a tone of disgust, "But this doesn't seem to have been our lucky night."

"What about the logs in the lagoon?" Chuck asked Tim.

The latter shrugged. "We managed to save two," he replied. "The others—four prime sticks—are scattered somewhere among these islands."

It wasn't good news, and yet the situation did not seem hopeless. "It'll be daylight soon," Chuck pointed out. "As soon as we have breakfast we can start searching for them, can't we?"

Tim nodded. "That's what we've planned," he said. "But the trouble is that Jarvis will also be out looking for sticks which have gone adrift during the night. A windstorm always means a harvest for him. The regular log patrol will be on the job, too, but they'll only pick up logs which belong to their customers, the big timber outfits. Jarvis is smart enough to leave such sticks alone. But he won't hesitate to grab *our* timber, as well as that of any other hand-logger who hasn't regular log patrol protection."

"Leastwise," ventured Gramps, "he'll be so busy that likely he won't bother our logs in the cove. We can be thankful for *that* much!"

Breakfast over, they set out just as day was breaking. Kamooks was told by Tim to stay behind with Gramps. Doc handled the engine; he usually operated it even when he and Chuck were alone together, as he had a knack of getting the most out of the small motor. For equipment they carried a maul, plenty of heavy spikes, and also several coils of rope.

Chuck learned that Tim and Doc had indeed put in a busy night, trying to keep the logs in the lagoon. Repeatedly the sticks had broken free, drifting away in the darkness. Pounded by waves and fighting across strong tidal currents, the boys had fought a losing battle in trying to recapture the sticks and tow them back to where they belonged. Only when the tide changed and the wind dropped had they met with much success. But, as Tim had already pointed out, four sticks had been lost, and possibly were now miles from Skookum-Chuck.

An hour's search along the waterways between the various islands produced none of the missing logs, although they found sticks which carried the brands of other owners. Then, as they rounded the headland of an island some five miles from Skookum-Chuck, they overhauled a big tug slowly towing a raft of a dozen or more sticks in the direction of the mainland.

"That's the regular log patrol," Tim explained. "They've already found some missing sticks—probably those belonging to the Sound Logging Company or some other big outfit," he added, with a brief glance at Chuck. "But you can bet that they won't bother to save any of *our* logs!" Then, as if regretting his bitterness, he said, "Not that I blame them. They can't afford to operate a big tug like that, with a crew of five or six men, for nothing—even to help out some poor hand-logger!"

Chuck made no comment. He knew that Tim was trying to be fair-minded. The pity of the situation was that the Elliotts couldn't afford to pay for the protection they needed against thieves like Jarvis. Nor could law authorities on the mainland help them. Jarvis was too crafty to be caught.

Tim called back to Doc, "Steer alongside that tug. I know the skipper, Bill Fuller; he's a friend of Gramps'. Maybe he's spotted some of our logs, even if he hasn't picked 'em up."

Doc obeyed. Soon the skiff was almost bumping the slow-moving tug dragging its log tow. A man leaned out of the wheelhouse window and waved. "That's Fuller," Tim announced. A deck hand came to the rail and tossed a line which Tim caught, and then the skiff was rubbing against the larger craft.

Bill Fuller, a big man with a weathered face which was creased in a friendly smile, came out of the wheelhouse and leaned over the rail. "Hi, Tim!" he greeted. "Lost some logs?"

"Four of them," the boy replied. "Did you see any of them?"

The big man nodded. "Three," he said. "There's one grounded on the beach on the far side of Clark Island," and he indicated the direction with his hand. "Another was drifting near Barnes Island. Third one was close inshore on the south side of Vendovi. But," and he wagged his head, "you may be a little late, Tim. I saw Jarvis' tug standing off Barnes Island when he stopped to see if the stick on the beach belonged to us. He probably moved in when we left."

Tim nodded understanding, his face gloomy. Jarvis had undoubtedly been log hunting since the first hint of daylight. He knew the currents among these islands, therefore the best spots to search for missing Elliott logs. His tug could move fast when it wasn't hampered by a log tow. Probably, too, he had watched Fuller's big tug; when the latter stopped, Jarvis knew that a drifting log had been spotted. If Fuller didn't take the stick in tow, Jarvis knew what to do.

"We'll go over to Clark, and take a look," Tim announced. "Thanks, Captain Fuller!"

"Wish I could help you, Tim," the log patrol man went on sympathetically, "but we've simply got our hands full, looking after the timber of our customers. But if there's any way by which you can catch Jarvis red-handed, you may count on me—and there'll be no charge. I've hoped to come on him with some of our logs, but he's too smart for that. Still, he may stumble one of these days, and if he does and I'm near enough to give you a hand, let me know. I'll do the best I can."

He gestured farewell. "Give my regards to Gramps!" he told Tim. Then Tim let go the line holding the skiff to the side of the tug, and Doc opened the throttle of the engine. Tim motioned in the direction he wished to go.

Clark Island was not large, but it was thickly wooded. With the engine turning over at top speed, the skiff sliced through the water, swinging wide to round a low point. Chuck stared straight ahead, half expecting to see Jarvis' tug lying off the beach. But there was no craft in sight.

Nor was there any log grounded on the beach, as the log patrol skipper had reported!

Doc slackened speed, and they cruised as close to shore as they dared go. The beach was clean and curving, and devoid of anything except a pair of crows walking along the sand in search of shellfish or some other food cast up by the sea. The water was glassy, save for a slight groundswell, an aftermath of the blow the previous night.

Suddenly Tim gave an exclamation and pointed ahead. Chuck looked. Bobbing in the lazy swell were two wooden cookies!

Tim shrugged hopelessly. "Beat us to it," he declared, "just as Fuller said Jarvis would. But let's take a closer look, and make sure."

Doc speeded up the motor, then slowed it again as they neared the flat blocks of wood. Soon they were alongside the first one. All three boys looked, then straightened up. There was no question about what had happened. On the upper side of the cookie the HE brand stood out clearly, just as Tim had hammered it into the wood with his branding maul the previous day. They didn't bother to look at the other disk; it had come from the opposite end of the stolen log.

Tim said in a tight voice, "Barnes Island next stop. Let's go—fast!" Doc obeyed, and with throttle wide open, they roared away on a new course.

Again they found they had come too late. Two more cookies were floating close to shore. Tim said, "That's Vendovi Island yonder," and indicated a land mass bigger than either Clark or Barnes. Once there they began cruising close to shore, but saw no missing log, not even a cookie.

At last Tim said, "It could have drifted away since Fuller spotted it. Maybe Jarvis missed it. He wouldn't dare take it in tow without cutting off the brand, and if he had we should be able to find at least one of the cookies. Might as well go someplace else and hunt for our logs."

But Chuck said, "Wait!" He pointed to a spot several hundred yards offshore. "See those gulls?" At least a dozen of the white birds were aligned in a row along the surface.

"Sure we see 'em!" Doc remarked impatiently. "What of it?"

Before Chuck could answer, Tim exclaimed, "I know what you mean! They're sitting on driftwood—*maybe one of our logs!*"

Doc stared, impressed. "What do you know?" he cried in an amazed tone. "Chuck, I apologize!" His hand twisted the throttle. "Let's go!"

The skiff seemed to fly over the water. With shrill cries of protest, the drowsing gulls rose in alarm and winged off. Expertly, Doc swerved the skiff alongside the floating object, and slowed the motor.

It was a log, all right, and as it turned slightly in the swell, the HE brand came into sight!

Tim grinned. "Jarvis overlooked this one," he declared. "Maybe we'll find the other." Then, as Doc held the skiff close alongside, Tim went to work.

The spike by which the stick had been moored to the float had evidently pulled out, but he produced another and drove it in place with the maul, looping a length of rope over it. Then, with the log in tow, they started back toward Skookum-Chuck.

A half-mile farther on, Tim's sharp eyes spotted another log; and this, too, was taken in tow.

Back in the lagoon once more, the recovered logs were secured, and Tim reported to Gramps what had been accomplished.

"You've done right well," the old man approved. "Better than I figured you'd do. Tim, I reckon we've got Chuck and Doc to thank for it. If it wasn't for that kicker-boat of theirs, you likely wouldn't have found any of the missin' sticks. Take you all day to row your skiff around these islands, and then you'd always be too late; Jarvis, with his tug, would probably have beaten you to every log we lost."

"Might as well give up," Tim decided. "We won't see those two other sticks again."

Chuck grinned. "Maybe we will!" he declared. "Have you forgotten that scheme of ours? Jarvis will take those logs directly to some mill on the mainland. All we have to do is find out where he sells them!"

Tim's eyes lit with interest. "Sure enough!" he exclaimed. "I *had* forgotten. Why," he added, "we already have our trap baited."

"What's this about a trap?" Gramps demanded.

Tim acted as if the matter were unimportant. "Just a little idea that Chuck and I have been working on," he explained. "No use bothering to tell you about it now, Gramps, because it may not be any good. But we'll have to make a trip to the mainland."

Gramps looked doubtful. "You be careful," he warned. "If I thought you aimed to get into a battle with Jarvis, I wouldn't let you go!"

Tim patted his shoulder. "Don't worry, Gramps," he assured the other. "We'll let Jarvis do the fighting, while we do the footwork!"

Chuck laughed at the hidden humor in Tim's words. It *would* be footwork—Tim's calk-marks on the logs—if they trapped Jarvis!

Doc seemed unimpressed, yet his eyes were alive with curiosity. "This sounds too good to be true," he said. "I have a *real* plan, or will have when I get through with my experiments. If you have a better one, it's something I want to see!"

"You're invited, of course," Chuck told him with mock gravity.

"Try to stop me!" Doc retorted.

The fuel tank of the outboard motor was filled for the long trip, and soon the power skiff, with the three boys aboard, went roaring out of the lagoon. Kamooks was left behind, not only to help guard the cabin but also as company for Gramps. As usual, Doc ran the motor, while Tim and Chuck sat side by side on a forward thwart. Because of the loud exhaust of the motor, Doc couldn't hear what they were saying. He tried to act as though he didn't care, yet he could not successfully hide the lively interest in his face.

Chuck leaned close to Tim and asked, "What's our first move?"

"We'll have to locate our stolen logs, of course," Tim replied, "and that may not be easy. There is no telling where Jarvis has sold them. Maybe he doesn't sell them to the same mill each time, but spreads them out among several buyers so as not to arouse suspicion over the fact that each of his logs is a little short, because he has sawed off the branded ends. I'm pretty certain none of these sawmill owners know what Jarvis is doing. They wouldn't want to be caught with stolen logs if the law finally catches up with Jarvis, which is bound to happen someday."

Chuck glanced aft, and he saw the strained look on Doc's face, as the latter tried to pick up a few words of what they were saying. But when Doc discovered that Chuck was watching him, he acted as though he didn't have the slightest interest in what they were talking about.

"We'll try Stinerson's mill first," Tim announced. "That's the nearest one. I've a hunch that Jarvis wouldn't tow the logs any farther than he has to." He signalled with his hands for Doc to change course slightly.

The exhaust of the little motor was a steady drumfire as the skiff raced onward over the smooth water.

Details of the mainland became clearer. Chuck saw the sawmill toward which they were headed, smoke rising from its tall stack while intermittent jets of steam came from an upright pipe. Tim waved his hand again, and once more the skiff changed course slightly until its prow was headed toward what appeared to be a log pond.

Now Chuck could make out the moving chain which carried logs up a wooden flume to the saw carriage, which in turn would send them ahead through the perpendicular band saws which would reduce each stick to boards, planks, and heavier timbers in almost a single operation. In the log pond three boom-men, armed with pike poles, moved over the rafted sticks, shoving the logs forward, one by one, until they were caught up by the toothed chain and hauled into the mill. Doc shut off the motor, and the craft slid alongside the outer boom.

Tim got out first and made the skiff's painter fast, then motioned for the boys to follow him. They obeyed, walking gingerly on the slippery logs, for only Tim had the secure footing which steel calks gave him.

The boom-men stopped work for a moment to regard them idly. Tim led the way across the sticks, and when they were near the foot of the slow-moving chain, a man came out of the mill and eyed them questioningly. "That's Ole Stinerson," Tim explained to the boys. "He's also an old-time logger, like Gramps."

Chuck gave an excited exclamation and pointed to

one of the sticks about to be caught up by the chain. "Look!" he cried. "There's one of your sticks, Tim. The HE brand you stamped on it is as plain as can be!"

"You're right!" Tim's voice was jubilant. "We're in luck, because we might have had to call at a dozen mills before finding one of our logs. I was right about Jarvis; he went straight for the nearest mill."

He swung around and faced the mill owner, and yelled, "Hey! Stop that log. It belongs to me!"

Ole Stinerson—elderly, yet big-framed and powerful-looking—looked astonished. "Tim Elliott!" he said in recognition. "What you talk about, boy? What you mean that log is yours? Is mine! I pay good money for it!"

Tim nodded impatiently, for the log had already been caught up by the chain and had begun its slow climb toward the waiting saws. "I know you did, Mr. Stinerson!" he cried. "But I cut that log, and it was stolen from me. I can prove it if you'll let me. Stop it before it reaches the saws!"

But the mill owner was not to be stampeded into action by such wild words from any mere boy. "Stolen?" His voice was incredulous. The log kept climbing.

"You bought it from Lem Jarvis, didn't you?" Tim demanded. Stinerson nodded. "Jarvis stole it from me!" Tim went on hurriedly.

The log reached the end of the chain. There it stopped. Then from below a massive wooden beam, its end protected by a sheath of heavy metal, came

127

up and almost as though it had human intelligence, began bumping the log toward the waiting saw carriage. As the log finally rolled in place on the carriage, the wooden beam sank back into the floor. The head sawyer on the carriage pulled a lever and steel "dogs" bit into the log, holding it firmly in place. Quickly he made adjustments that would enable him to fashion the log into the kind of lumber it was best suited to produce. Then the saw carriage began to move forward.

"Stop the mill before that log is cut!" begged Tim. "I'll prove to you that the log was stolen from me!"

But Stinerson merely smiled tolerantly. Stopping any unit of the mill meant idle men. "You talk foolishness, boy," he reminded Tim.

Tim groaned in frustration. Saw carriage and log reached the fast-traveling steel bands edged with sharp teeth, and from them rose a whine of exultation as they bit into the wood, a steady stream of sawdust pouring from the log as it was shoved forward.

"There goes our only chance!" he told Chuck and Doc. He faced the mill owner. "Mr. Stinerson," he told the latter, "if you'd only waited a few minutes I could have proved it was my log. It has my brand all over it!"

Stinerson wagged his blond head in disbelief. "How can that be?" he asked. "Before I buy that log, I look him over careful, you betcha! He has Jarvis' LJ brand at each end!"

"What of it?" Tim insisted. "Sure, you found his brand. He sawed off the end of each stick, so as to remove my brand and stamped his own on it. It's an old log pirate trick."

He turned to Chuck and Doc. "Well," he said disgustedly, "we might as well go home!"

But the mill owner, although his mind might be slowmoving, had a stubborn streak in him; when he once grasped an idea, he wouldn't let go readily. Likewise, he might have been impressed by the genuine look of concern in Tim's face.

"Tim," he said a bit chidingly, "this is wild, strange talk you make. I do not like it said that I buy stolen logs. You wait here. I find out about this pretty quick, you betcha!" He turned and vanished inside the mill.

The boys looked at each other, mystified. "What does he mean?" Chuck asked. "What is he going to do?"

Tim shrugged. "Who can tell? But we'll stick around. He's worried, all right, but not convinced that I'm telling the truth. Maybe he's thought of a way to find out."

Doc said almost casually, trying to keep curiosity out of his voice, "Maybe if you geniuses explained to me what you're trying to do, I could help. Good old Doc Peters seldom fails, you know!"

Chuck looked at Tim. "Might as well tell him," Chuck suggested. Tim nodded.

They explained how Tim had used his calked boots to brand each Elliott log. Doc nodded understanding.

"Very clever," he approved. "Almost brilliant, I might say. But," he added disparagingly, *"something tells me it won't work!*

"The situation," he went on, with his usual pretense of superiority, "calls for the well-known Play Twenty-Two—and I'll have that perfected when we get back to the island. Next time you geniuses come up with what you think is a good idea, you'd better call in an expert and have it analyzed!"

Chuck felt annoyed, even though he knew Doc was merely trying to add a little satirical humor to what he understood well enough was a serious situation. Doc liked to joke—yet sometimes he went too far! "Well, Mr. Brains," Chuck told him sarcastically, "maybe you'll let us in on *your* big secret, now that you've decided ours won't work!"

"In due time," Doc replied loftily. "In due time!" Chuck felt like roughhousing him.

Yet just then Stinerson came out of the mill, and hurried down to the log pond, where he beckoned to the nearest boom-man. The mill owner spoke rapidly to the other, and the latter nodded. Then the boom-man rejoined the others, and the three of them began moving over the raft as though searching for something.

Stinerson came up to where the boys were waiting. There was quiet triumph in his manner. "We get this straightened out quick," he announced. "You get chance, Tim, to prove if what you say is true!"

"How?" Tim asked. "You've cut up the stick that was evidence!"

"Ah, so I did!" Stinerson agreed with a smile. "But you forget, boy, that there is *another* stick which I buy from Jarvis today. I buy *two* logs! He bring

130

them here not over two hours ago. Because they are last logs to arrive, there has not been time to cut them. My men find another LJ log for you, Tim. Then you have your chance. Is fair?"

Tim's face was wreathed in a sudden smile. "Sure! I'd forgotten about the other stick. Why," he exulted, "this is going to be easy! Thanks, Mr. Stinerson. Just show me one of those LJ logs!"

The mill owner nodded. "Soon, I think," he replied. "But first we wait for Lem Jarvis!"

"Jarvis?" Tim was startled.

Again the mill owner nodded. "But yes! His tug is tied up at the fish wharf only a half-mile from here. I telephone watchman there, and he call Jarvis. I tell Jarvis to come here in big hurry—that I want to ask him about those logs. He come quick, I betcha!"

9 . . . Face-to-Face

*T*he boys eyed each other uneasily. This was more than they had expected! Lem Jarvis was coming! What would happen when he confronted them? What would he do if they actually proved that the logs he had sold to Stinerson had been stolen from Tim Elliott? What would Stinerson do?

The mill owner, for all his stolid temperament, was a man of action once he was aroused. Jarvis, Chuck thought, wasn't exactly a cream puff, either. What would Jarvis do if Tim proved he was a thief?

But it was useless to do any guessing. Jarvis might not show up at all. His own guilt might make him suspicious of a trap. Yet if he refused to appear, as Stinerson had requested, he would be practically admitting his guilt. And that would end his log-thieving operations on Puget Sound, because the word would spread rapidly and no mill owner would dare buy timber from him hereafter. No, Chuck decided, Lem Jarvis would surely appear!

132

Stinerson and the boys faced toward the log pond as one of the boom-men called out, "Here's an LJ stick!"

"Bring in it close!" Stinerson ordered, "and be sure to keep it away from the chain." To the boys he added, "I take good look at that log, you betcha!"

Tim made no answer. But Chuck could guess what Tim was thinking—that everything depended on this showdown. Of a sudden, it seemed to Chuck, the plan which he and Tim had worked out, and which had seemed so sound, now appeared to be almost childish. Doc had said it wouldn't work. Chuck thought a little angrily, *how does he know, anyway?* The thing *might* succeed!

Presently Stinerson remarked quietly, "Here comes Jarvis' tug!"

Chuck followed the gaze of the mill owner and saw the familiar, dark-hulled craft rounding a nearby point. Just as Chuck had expected, Jarvis had lost no time in accepting Stinerson's challenge. Maybe, too, his curiosity had been aroused. He wanted to know what was up, what the Elliotts were doing. Apparently he was bold enough to feel confident that he could bluff his way through any sort of situation.

On the other hand, Chuck could not help looking forward to the meeting with a sort of eager anticipation. It was a natural curiosity, for he wanted a look at the man who was back of all the trouble that had befallen the Elliotts, no matter what the outcome would be.

As the tug neared rapidly, Chuck saw a tall figure

standing on deck forward of the wheelhouse. Lem Jarvis, undoubtedly. On that day of the storm, when Chuck and Doc had met the tug outside the cove on Skookum-Chuck, it had been impossible to make out clearly the features of the log pirate, because of the driving rain and the spume from wind-whipped waves. Yet there was something familiar about the man on the foredeck of the tug; unless Chuck was mistaken, *this* was the rifleman who had fired the warning shot over the heads of the two boys in the skiff.

The tug bumped alongside the boomed logs, a deck hand dropped to the sticks and made the craft fast, and then the tall man came striding across the raft to where Stinerson and the boys waited.

He stopped at last, just in front of them, and Chuck eyed him with interest. Lem Jarvis was above average height, and he was lean and muscular. By the sure-footedness with which he had walked over the boomed logs, it was plain that his boots were calked; also, that he was used to floating timber. A red hat, almost the standard mark of a logger, was jammed on the back of his head. A stubble of black beard covered his jaws; his eyes were deep-sunken, yet bright with suspicion. Here was a man, Chuck decided instantly, who was not only dangerous but cunning as well.

"What's on your mind, Stinerson?" Jarvis asked abruptly. "You sounded as though you're worried. Said you wanted to ask me about them logs I sold you."

Stinerson nodded, and indicated the boys with a

wave of his hand. "You know Tim Elliott, maybe," he remarked. "These boys his friends, I guess."

"So what?" Jarvis voice was impatient. Yet at the same time his eyes were busy as he sized up Chuck and Doc. Maybe he was thinking rather contemptuously, *Nothing but a pair of kids! So they're all I have to worry about!* His gaze went back to Stinerson.

"Tim Elliott, here," said the mill owner, "claim the logs you sold me today were stolen from him. What's more, he say he prove it!"

Jarvis' eyes widened. Then he smiled patronizingly. "Prove it?" he demanded harshly. "What's he talkin' about, anyway? I cut them logs myself— leastwise my woods crew did. They came from Lopez Island, them sticks did. Guess I ought to know; cost me enough money by the time I got 'em towed to your mill, Stinerson!"

The three boys stared at him. Chuck felt amazed at the calm assurance of the man. To be sure, Lem Jarvis was a liar, yet he was a most convincing one. If Chuck hadn't known the truth, he would, he admitted to himself, have been inclined to believe what Jarvis was saying. No wonder he had been able to make mill owners believe that he was an honest logger!

Jarvis' voice took on almost an injured tone. "You mean to say," he asked Stinerson, "that you'd take the word of this kid against mine? You know as well as I do that kids are always dreamin' up some yarn because they get a kick out of it. It ain't right," he concluded, his voice big with indignation, "for kids to be runnin' around sayin' things that ain't so! If I had a boy and he'd do a thing like that, I'd tan the hide off'n him!"

Stinerson was silent. It was plain to Chuck that the mill owner was impressed by Jarvis' straightforward manner. At the same time, Ole Stinerson wasn't exactly a fool; also, he wasn't quick to get rid of an idea, once that one came to him.

"Well," asked Jarvis brusquely, "do you believe me, Stinerson, or do you believe that kid?" and he indicated Tim.

Stinerson shrugged. "I believe nothing—yet," he replied. "All I want is to be sure I am not handling stolen logs. We find out quick, I betcha!"

He turned to Tim, and his voice was cold. "Well, now," he suggested, "you make big talk, boy. Maybe you prove what you say. Go ahead. I'm waiting!"

He pointed to the stick which the boom-men had sorted from among the others. "There," he declared, "is one of the sticks I buy from Jarvis. It has his LJ brand on it. You show me it is yours!"

Tim took a deep breath and walked over to the log, studied the bark on the upper side, for it still floated in the same position as when he had stamped his calk-marks on it. He pointed to the pattern of tiny holes in the outer wood. "I purposely walked back and forth on this stick after I'd bucked the tree into logs," he explained. He lifted his right foot and showed the HE design of the calks. "I fixed my calks this way so that the logs would be double-branded, so they could still be identified even after Jarvis had sawed off the ends. Maybe he didn't notice what I'd

136

done, or he'd have also peeled off the bark from the upper side of the stick!"

Stinerson frowned in amazement; apparently he had never heard of such a thing as this. Yet Jarvis, his face working with anger and astonishment, shouted, "Why, that's crazy nonsense, Stinerson! Nobody but a fool would believe such a yarn!"

Chuck saw that Jarvis had made a mistake. The mill owner's features hardened. "I do not like to be called a fool," he told Jarvis.

"I didn't call you one," Jarvis declared hastily. "I only said that anybody who'd believe such a thing was a fool!"

Yet Stinerson was only partially mollified. "Why *shouldn't* I believe it?" he asked.

"Because," the other declared, "you can see what really happened. This kid," and he indicated Tim, "is tryin' to get me in bad with you mill owners. So he found a raft of my logs and, when I wasn't lookin' —maybe at night—he stomped his brand on the sticks, just so he could claim I stole the timber. Can't you see *that?*"

Stinerson nodded, and Chuck felt his own spirits take a nose-dive. "Jarvis," the man said, "what you say could be true. It is hard to decide. Tim," and he faced the boy, "you have not proved your point. It could have happened as Jarvis said it did. I do not say it *did* happen that way, mind you, but it *could* have. Even if I believed you, such evidence as you have would not hold up in any court, I betcha!"

Tim looked downcast. "I suppose you're right, Mr.

Stinerson," he agreed. "All I can say here is that I didn't brand any logs that weren't my own. My friends, here, will back me up!"

"Yah, sure," Stinerson said. "Maybe you are telling truth. I hope so. But I am talking about *proof, boy!* It is your word against that of Lem Jarvis. Who can decide?"

"Stinerson," Jarvis asserted jubilantly, "you've got more sense than I thought you had. You—"

But it was plain that Jarvis had not chosen his words well.

"Yet I am not finished!" the mill owner interrupted him angrily. "You think I am big fool, maybe. All right, now, I tell you this: *I believe Tim Elliott is telling truth!* What you say to that, hah?"

He took a step nearer the log pirate. "I tell you more," he went on. *"From now on, I buy no more logs from you!* Whether you are honest man, or whether you are log pirate, I do not say; but I have my own ideas, I betcha! Hereafter, you sell your logs some other place. Understand?"

Jarvis was plainly taken aback, yet he managed to force a bleak smile of scorn. "If that's the way you want it," he retorted, "that's the way it'll be! Plenty of other mills where I can sell my logs. And if I hear that you're peddlin' stories to other mill owners that you won't buy any more logs from me because you figure I stole 'em, then I'll haul you into court for slander and maybe take this mill away from you!"

Stinerson clenched his work-hardened fists. "Get off my property!" he shouted. "And stay off! I tell my men to watch out for you. Maybe you try to steal *my* logs some night! You do that, and I break you up into little pieces!"

Jarvis backed away, yet his grin was defiant. "Don't worry," he replied. "I'll keep away from your mill—and so will everybody else that has any logs to sell, if I have anything to say about it. Maybe before long you'll be so short of logs that you'll have to shut down!" He turned and started back toward his waiting tug.

"If I have to saw stolen logs," Stinerson called after him, "then I quit this business in a hurry, I betcha!"

Tim said, "I'm sorry, Mr. Stinerson, to have been the cause of this row, but I really told you the truth about Jarvis stealing my logs."

"I know you did," the other replied. "Me, I think I should give these logs back to you, even if I do lose what I have already paid for them. I do that, I betcha!"

"No!" Tim's voice was firm. "Gramps wouldn't have it that way, and neither would I. It was our loss, not yours. Anyway, Mr. Stinerson, you've done us a big favor as it is—you've broken with Jarvis, and won't buy any more of his logs. Gramps will be happy to learn what you've done."

"I try to be honest," Stinerson declared. "I do not like that Lem Jarvis, and never did. I don't care what he say he will do, I tell other mill owners to look out for him."

He put a fatherly hand on Tim's shoulder. "You

139

good boy," he said. "You have good friends," and he nodded to Chuck and Doc. "I hope you lick this Lem Jarvis." Then he turned and went back into the mill.

Somewhat disconsolately, the boys got into the skiff, and Doc prepared to start the engine. "Might as well go home," Tim decided. "Jarvis was too smart for us. Stinerson is okay. He tried to be fair. As he pointed out, we couldn't prove anything against Jarvis. Anyway, we tried, although we lost!"

"Maybe we won't lose next time," Doc predicted seriously. "All joking aside, I believe my plan will work, and if it does it won't be a matter of taking anybody's word. The proof will be there—in plain sight!"

"Just what *is* this airtight scheme of yours?" Chuck asked with a touch of sarcasm.

Doc grinned at him. Once more Doc was back in his usual form, putting on an act. "Wait and see, bud," he replied, with an exaggerated wink. "Wait and see!" Then, before Chuck could retort, Doc spun the flywheel. The little motor roared in response, and the skiff began heading homeward.

Nobody attempted conversation; each seemed busy with his own thoughts. One thing was certain, Chuck decided: the war with Lem Jarvis was on in earnest. They had spoiled one of his markets for stolen logs; that was an act of aggression he could scarcely overlook. He'd had opportunity now to size up Tim's allies; he understood the nature of his opposition. Only three boys to worry about! It was going to be next to impossible to trick him in the future as they had done in the past. It seemed that Jarvis' confidence had been strengthened as his cunning brain weighed the situation; he hadn't been entirely defeated in his clash with Stinerson, but probably had gained something. Chuck sensed that real trouble lay ahead.

As the skiff raced onward the islands of the San Juan group grew more distinct. In this calm weather there was plenty of shipping in sight—pleasure cruisers, sports fishermen, a huge oil tanker bound inward for some Puget Sound port, a rusty freighter headed out toward the Strait of Juan de Fuca, a tug pushing a heavily laden barge. Tim pointed to starboard. "There's the log patrol," he announced. "Fuller's tug is coming this way. I'd like to tell him what happened at Stinerson's mill."

He gestured to Doc, who changed course so that distance between it and the log patrol craft began to shorten. As the two neared, the tug began to lose headway, Fuller apparently recognizing the skiff and understanding that it wished to come alongside. Doc swung the skiff to make a curving approach, and soon it was bobbing beside the bigger boat.

"Find all your logs?" Fuller called to Tim.

Tim shook his head. "All but two, and Jarvis got those." Then he described the attempt they had made to identify the stolen sticks at Stinerson's mill. Fuller smiled.

"It was a good idea," he declared, "even if it didn't work. But I'm not surprised that Jarvis proved too slick for a trick like that. Anyway," he continued, "now that Stinerson is aroused, maybe other mill owners will get suspicious of the logs Jarvis offers for sale. He might find the situation so unprofitable that he will move to other hunting grounds. Not that I'd like to see him go; I'd prefer to have him stay and get caught, as he surely will someday. But my guess is that he won't leave this part of the country, because he must be pretty sure now that there is no legal way to prove he is a thief."

"He's probably right," Tim declared bitterly.

"But I'm going to have a talk with the authorities about the situation," Fuller went on. "Of course, there is not much they can do in the way of protecting small loggers like your grandfather and yourself; you could hardly expect them to station guards on Skookum-Chuck Island, for example. But Sheriff Jim Dunham is a good friend of mine, and he'll listen to me. And if Jarvis ever makes his one big mistake, the sheriff will already be informed and will act fast. Meanwhile, I'll keep an eye on Jarvis as much as possible."

"Thanks!" Tim said gratefully. "Gramps and I will appreciate anything you can do for us!"

Fuller waved his hand in farewell, and the tug got underway as the skiff turned away and once more headed for Skookum-Chuck. Soon it was tied up at the wharf in the lagoon, and the boys were at the cabin.

Gramps had little to say after Tim reported the result of the trip to the mainland. But he did remark mournfully, "Two good logs would have helped a lot toward your schooling, Tim! And Lem Jarvis stole 'em! Seems like justice has died out of this world!"

"We're not licked until we admit it, Gramps," Tim declared stoutly. "Next time luck may be on *our* side!"

"Sayin' so doesn't make it so," the old man insisted stubbornly. Then resentment filled his voice. "If I could only get around like I used to! I'd bet Lem Jarvis wouldn't dare come within rifle shot of this island!"

"Easy, Gramps!" Tim urged consolingly. "No use worrying about something that can't be helped. We'll keep on cutting logs, and Jarvis will keep on stealing most of them. But maybe some day he'll take the wrong stick!"

"That's a promise!" Doc said with quiet firmness.

Chuck looked at him. There was serious confidence in Doc's manner. No matter how much Doc enjoyed acting mysteriously important at times, Chuck knew and understood such byplay; and Chuck likewise knew that when Doc Peters was in deadly earnest about doing a thing, he usually did it. *He's not fooling now,* Chuck decided. *The guy must really have something!*

Of a sudden Chuck felt confident, too. He only wished that he could make Gramps and Tim feel the same way, yet he realized that they didn't know Doc as he did. Regrettable, too, was the fact that until Doc got good and ready, he wasn't going to spoil the dramatic moment of his triumph—whatever it was— by any advance information.

Tim suggested, "There's still a good part of the day left. Want to cut some more logs?"

"Good idea," Chuck approved. "What do you say, Doc?"

"You hairy-chested woodsmen go right ahead," was the reply. "I have important work of my own to do. But when you get ready to brand the ends of the new logs, Tim, I'd like to have you do it a certain way. Can do?"

"Anything you say, mister," Tim replied shortly. "Anything you say!"

As he and Chuck left the cabin and started up the hillside to the scene of the logging operation, Tim remarked, "Guess I'll never understand Doc very well. I like him a lot, of course, but most of the time he puzzles me."

Chuck laughed reassuringly. "Don't try to understand him! He may sound as though he's talking through his hat, but long ago I learned that with him it's only an act. If he says that he is going to do a thing, then you'd better believe that he can!"

"You really think he's cooked up a way to trap Lem Jarvis?"

Chuck nodded. "I don't know how Doc will do it," he replied, "or when he'll do it, but you can be sure he knows what he's talking about. That boy has picked up a lot of odds and ends of the queerest information you ever heard about—stuff that the average fellow wouldn't waste time with. Doc might be a scientist some day. At least he's going to be a great quarterback at college, a real field general."

"I can believe that," Tim agreed. "But when it comes to beating Lem Jarvis—"

"I'll still bet on Doc!" Chuck broke in.

There was only time left that day to cut down one more tree, send it shooting down the hillside, and buck it into three logs. Doc was on hand when it came time for Tim to mark the sticks by means of the branding maul.

"Swing that maul as hard as you can," he directed. "Hit the log hard so that the brand will be driven in deeply. And brand it in several different places. That's important!"

Tim obeyed. There was no use in asking Doc why he was making the strange request. When the job was finished, Doc squinted at the ends of the logs, and nodded approval.

"That'll do it," he declared.

The others said nothing, but looked at him expectantly.

"I'm taking the first patrol tonight," he went on. "Got a job to do in the cove. I'm going to brand all the logs you have left there."

"But they're already branded," Tim pointed out.

"Not the way I want 'em," Doc returned. "I'll take the branding maul with me in the skiff."

A half-hour later he was on his way. Chuck stared at Doc and the skiff as the sturdy little craft vanished around the nearest point, bound for the cove. For some reason which he could not have explained, Chuck felt a twinge of uneasiness.

Tim, aware of the sober look on the boy's face,

asked, "What's wrong? You act as though you're worried!"

Chuck shrugged his shoulders. "Maybe I am," he admitted.

"About what?"

"I don't know," Chuck confessed. "Just a hunch, I guess. But I can't help feeling that Doc is headed for trouble tonight. It may be that I can't forget the way Jarvis acted when he had that row with Stinerson. Jarvis blames us for that, of course. He's going to square accounts, if he can. And if he decides that tonight is the time to do it, Doc will be running straight into trouble. That's what is worrying me, I guess."

Tim said nothing, yet his face was sober. In silence the two boys walked slowly toward the cabin.

10 ... Battle of the Night

*A*s darkness came, an unusual, almost an ominous, quiet settled over those in the cabin. Seated in his old chair by the window, Gramps had nothing to say. He may have been pondering what had happened, what it could mean in the future. As for Chuck and Tim, they had little to talk about. Possibly their thoughts mainly concerned Doc, alone out there in the night, keeping watch over the logs in the cove.

The uneasiness which Chuck had mentioned to Tim seemed to be felt by all. Even Kamooks, ordinarily content to lie before the open fire, was affected, for from time to time he got up from his accustomed place and padded restlessly about the room, only to return to the hearth.

Time dragged—an hour, two hours, three. At last Chuck got up and went outside, staring up at the night sky. A half-moon hung in the blue-black heavens; the air was still. From the shore of the lagoon

147

came a weird, croaking cry, which he guessed was made by a big blue heron night-hunting along the shallows. After awhile he went back inside, and said to Tim, "Seems to me Doc should be back by this time. When he does return, I'll relieve him and take the next watch, if it's okay with you."

Tim nodded agreement. "Maybe Doc has spotted Jarvis' tug," he said almost hopefully, "and doesn't want to leave the cove until he is certain that the logs are safe. No danger in that. Anyway, you'll remember that he has some work of his own to do—rebranding those logs. He took the branding maul with him, as he said he'd do."

"Suppose that's it," Chuck replied. "Still, I don't like it. He's overdue at least half an hour. He *might* be in trouble!"

Gramps spoke up suddenly, "Don't like it myself, boys. Got a sort of hunch that somethin's gone wrong."

"Rebranding the logs wouldn't take long," Chuck reasoned.

Tim got up and walked about the room. "We'll wait a half-hour," he decided. "Then, if he hasn't showed up, we'll walk to the cove and find out what is delaying him. If he's okay, then we'll save time in keeping the patrol going because you, Chuck, can take over the skiff, and Doc can walk home with me. In that way it won't be necessary to run the boat back here to the lagoon."

Chuck nodded emphatic approval. Tim's suggestion relieved the tension. At least they'd find out what was going on. It meant action of a sort, which was far better than merely sitting here, waiting.

The minutes slid by. Kamooks got restless again, and went to the door and scratched on it. Yet when Chuck opened the panel, the big wolf-dog did not go outside; instead, he stood there, head lifted, sniffing the slow-moving currents of air flowing down the hillside back of the cabin.

"Got wind of somethin'," Gramps decided. He peered out the window beside him. "Can't be that Jarvis has landed on Skookum-Chuck and is tryin' to sneak up on us!" His voice sounded disbelieving, yet Chuck found his words startling.

"If Jarvis has landed," Tim remarked, "he can't be close, or Kamooks would really let us know! Bet he can smell a stranger or log pirate a mile away! Probably he's just uneasy about something he doesn't understand, but sort of senses."

"He's got wolf-blood in him," Gramps remarked, "and I reckon a wolf has instincts which us humans don't know a thing about."

The old man's manner became abrupt. "Tim," he declared, "I reckon we've waited long enough. You and Chuck best light out for the cove. And take Kamooks with you! I'll make out fine here, alone. That dog might prove useful to you, for all we know."

Chuck was grateful. It seemed to him that he couldn't have stood the suspense much longer. Likewise, Gramps' suggestion appeared to suit Tim. "Let's go!" he said to Chuck.

To Gramps he said, "We'll hurry back and let you know as soon as we find out what has happened. Sure you'll be all right alone? Maybe it would be better if the dog stayed behind!"

"Get started!" exclaimed Gramps. "Take the dog with you, as I said. Anyway, he wouldn't stay behind unless you chained him up. He's rarin' to go!"

This was obviously true. The sudden activity told Kamooks all he wanted to know; the boys were going somewhere! He whined in eager approval, wagging his fluffy tail. "Come on, then!" Tim told him, opening the door. But the invitation wasn't needed; Kamooks pushed past him and led the way into the night. He immediately headed up the trail which led over the hill to the cove.

Tim followed him, and Chuck came last. The moonlight was strong enough to reveal the way, and they walked briskly. Yet after a few hundred yards Tim halted, and so did Chuck, and they stood there together, listening.

In the stillness which lay over the island, the sound of an outboard motor should carry far; it seemed to them that they ought to have heard the power skiff from the time it left the cove until Doc shut off the engine at the lagoon. Yet they heard nothing. Something's surely wrong, Chuck told himself as they started on once more.

Even when they topped the ridge and paused again to listen, the silence persisted. Kamooks trotted ahead, as though impatient. The boys went on, quickening their pace. Down the slope they moved rapidly, until at last they could see the cove, which in the moonlight seemed like a steel mirror. Nor did they pause until they reached its shore.

There was no sign of the skiff, or Doc. Tim peered at the log-raft behind the boom. "I can't be sure," he remarked, "but it seems like some sticks are missing."

"Then Jarvis *has* been here!" Chuck exclaimed.

"Afraid so," was the reply. "But where is Doc?"

There was no immediate answer to that, of course. "Let's see if we can find his tracks in this sand," Tim suggested. "He probably landed in here, someplace."

They moved along the curving beach, but found no V-shaped mark such as would have been made by the keel of the skiff. In so doing, they neared the log-raft where the boomsticks almost touched the shore. Chuck pointed to the water farther out. "Something floating there," he remarked. "Looks like several cookies."

Tim looked. "They *are* cookies," he decided. "That makes it certain Jarvis has been here tonight and stolen some of the logs." Then he repeated his previous question, "But where is Doc?"

Chuck made no reply, but his gaze went back along the shore they had been following. "Kamooks is gone," he announced.

Tim swung around abruptly, puzzled. "Now, what's happened to *him?*" he complained. "He wouldn't leave us unless he's found something we've missed."

He turned back. "Come on!" Tim urged. "We've

got to find him. Maybe he can tell us what has happened to Doc!"

Tim led the way, retracing their steps to the point where they had left the trail which twisted down the hillside. The tracks of the wolf-dog were plain. For a short distance he had followed the boys; then, for some reason of his own, he had turned back. Tim, with Chuck close behind, took up the new trail.

It moved almost in a straight line toward the mouth of the cove; then, just before the rocky entrance was reached, it swung to the left and continued down the outer shore of the island. "Why not call him?" Chuck suggested. But Tim shook his head negatively.

"We don't know what we might be running into," he pointed out. "Jarvis and his men might have landed on the island, and may still be here. Let's go easy until we find out what the situation is. If we don't catch up with Kamooks soon, maybe he'll start hunting for us instead."

For a short distance, then, the dog's trail became hard to follow, because it crossed a wide patch of bare rock; but soon it showed again in the sand of the beach. By and by a rocky point loomed ahead, and beyond this they could not see. As they started to climb it, both boys stopped, frozen.

From up ahead came a wailing cry, the drawn-out call of a wolf. "Kamooks!" Chuck exclaimed.

For an instant the boy felt terror such as he had never known before. It wasn't fear for his own safety; it was dread at what the wolf-call could mean.

Death? He had heard that even dogs sometimes voice the woe in their souls in telling whoever can hear them that they have made a dread discovery. A wolf, he reasoned, probably would do the same thing. *Doc!* he thought. *Kamooks is trying to tell us to hurry!*

Tim's voice was strangely comforting, as though he understood the fear which had gripped his companion. "Don't be worried," he advised. "That's only Kamooks' way of telling us that he's found something interesting. Let's see what it is!"

Chuck didn't need any urging to go on. The boys fairly raced up the rocky slope, and down the other side, and then they glimpsed something in the moonlight a hundred yards or more down the beach. It was the skiff, partly drawn up on shore, with Kamooks squatting beside it, his nose pointed toward the sky. Once more he sent that quavering, blood-chilling cry into the still night.

They reached the boat within a few seconds. First they looked inside it, and Chuck dreaded what they might see. But Doc wasn't there; everything seemed to be in order. The branding maul was missing, but the oars were stowed in their usual place, fore and aft beneath the thwarts, and the outboard motor was clamped to the stern. The bowline of the skiff had been carried ashore, and one end tied to a heavy piece of driftwood. There was no sign that a struggle had occurred here. Far from being solved, the mystery was more puzzling than ever.

But Tim, in his practical way, tried to put some

153

pieces of the story together. "Doc must have landed here," he deduced, "and tied the skiff. Then he went somewhere on the island." He eyed Kamooks. The wolf-dog still sat there, *facing seaward!* Again he voiced his wolfish summons.

"That's funny," Tim remarked. "He keeps looking out yonder," and he indicated the sweep of water away from the island. "Surely Doc didn't leave the boat and go swimming!"

"Hey!" cried Chuck. "I've found Doc's tracks!"

He pointed to the sand. There were footprints, and certainly not made by the boots of a logger. They led back toward the cove.

Tim gave an exclamation of chagrin. "Wonder why I didn't notice those sooner! The story is getting plainer. He landed here, for some good reason, and decided to walk to the cove instead of going by boat. But why?"

"Probably it had something to do with the log pirates," Chuck guessed. "Maybe he had spotted Jarvis' tug standing off the cove. As usual, Jarvis' skiff would take a couple of men into the cove to tow the logs out. Maybe Doc figured that if he went in there after them, in the power skiff, they might trap him. The tug could box him in at the entrance; the men in the skiff would keep him from landing and getting away to warn us. He didn't want to take those chances, so he got out here and walked to the cove, planning to surprise them and make them think all three of us were there, waiting in ambush."

"Sounds as though it could have happened that

way," Tim agreed. "But what happened to him after that? We didn't meet him on the trail over the hill, and we didn't find him at the cove. He couldn't have disappeared into thin air!"

"Listen!" Chuck admonished.

Tim obeyed. From out at sea beyond the mouth of the cove there came sudden sounds—angry cries, shouting. The moonlight wasn't strong, yet it seemed to the boys that they could make out the shadowy bulk of some fairly large craft, either hove-to or at anchor. Faintly they heard a man's voice, "Get him next time he comes up! 'Way over there to starboard! You numbskulls better make a job of it!" There was something familiar about the voice. Jarvis!

The boys faced each other, exclaiming in unison, "Doc!" Then Tim added quickly, "That's Jarvis' tug yonder. His skiff must be there, too. Hear those oars splashing?

"Doc's in the water! *They're after him!*"

Chuck declared, "Then they must have captured him at the cove after all. But he got away from them. Now he's swimming toward shore. It isn't far to the beach from where the tug is lying!"

"What are we waiting for?" Tim demanded. "Jump into the skiff, and let's go!"

It took only a moment. While Tim untied the rope securing the skiff to the driftwood, Chuck hurried aft to the engine. Then, as Tim put his shoulder against the bow and gave a mighty heave which sent the skiff backward into deeper water, then himself scrambling aboard, Chuck yanked the starter rope.

At the same instant Kamooks took a running leap and landed in the bottom of the skiff; he was determined that he wasn't going to be left behind.

The engine fired instantly. Chuck let it warm up only for a few seconds, then opened the throttle and swung the skiff around until it was headed in the direction where those cries had come.

The skiff fairly leaped over the water. Soon the shape of the tug, apparently anchored, became clearer. They were within gunshot, Chuck realized, and Jarvis certainly had a rifle. But there was no time now to worry about what might happen. Doc needed help!

Presently Tim cried, "I see him! Jarvis' skiff, too." He had to yell loudly to make himself heard, but Chuck understood. Chuck also could see Jarvis' boat, two men in it, each manning a pair of oars. A hundred yards ahead of Jarvis' skiff the silvery surface of the water had broken.

What looked like an arm was lifted for an instant; then it vanished. Immediately the two-man skiff turned that way, but the water was smoothing out at the spot which Chuck had observed.

His throat tightened at realization of what it might mean. Doc had gone under! *Was he drowning?* Chuck's right hand twisted the throttle open still more, and the skiff almost planed over the water, heading straight toward Jarvis' skiff!

Up in the bow Tim nodded understanding approval. Collision! *That* was the way! Tim reached under the thwart and pulled out the oars, shoving one

156

aft until it was within the reach of Chuck, if the latter wanted to use it. "Smash 'em!" Tim shouted. "Hit 'em amidships, if you can. Then slug 'em with the oars!"

Tim was fighting mad. For one berserk moment he was truly the grandson of tempestuous old "High Explosive" Elliott. Remembrance of all the grief and trouble these heartless log pirates had caused him and his grandfather rose up devastatingly inside him. Moreover, he would battle to save the life of his friend, helplessly struggling there in the chill water.

Intuitively, Chuck understood the impulses which had aroused Tim. Driven by the gunned motor, the power skiff shot true as an arrow toward the other craft. There was no time for Chuck to count cost. The impact might splinter both boats, sink them. Any second, too, there might come a bullet from the rifle of Lem Jarvis, out on the tug. The risks, grave though they were, had to be taken.

For the first time, then, the men in the skiff seemed aware of the disaster racing toward them. Apparently they had been so interested in overtaking the swimming boy that they had failed to hear or see the oncoming power skiff. But now, realizing their danger, they acted quickly.

From broadside, they swung their boat around until its stern faced the power skiff. Chuck saw the reason for the maneuver. They were going to wait until the last second before the crash, then suddenly pull clear, dodging to right or left.

There was no telling which direction they would

go. The power skiff was now traveling so fast that it could not be turned abruptly from its course. The distance between the two boats shortened rapidly. Now only a few feet separated them. With the sharp prow of the power skiff aimed at the stern of the other craft, Chuck leaned forward to brace himself against the shock.

He saw the other skiff turn left, the men pulling frantically. But they were not quick enough; the power skiff was going too fast. Tim crouched, gripping his oar in readiness to use as a club. Even Kamooks sensed what was coming, for he flattened himself in the bottom of the skiff.

Chuck tensed himself, closed his eyes.

There was a shuddering jar that half lifted himself from the stern seat; the sound of splintering wood, terrified yells from the men in the other boat. He opened his eyes to see the prow of their skiff slice into a corner of the other craft, saw the latter split apart. The power skiff stopped momentarily, then shot ahead again, clear of the log pirates' craft.

One man had seized an oar and aimed a blow at Tim as the skiff swept past. But Tim parried the blow, and struck back, the oar blade glancing off the man's shoulder. Then, as the skiff picked up speed and passed abeam of the foe, Chuck saw that the opposing boat was filling rapidly. So far as he could tell, their own skiff was undamaged.

He had an impulse to turn and ram the enemy again, finishing the battle, but at that moment he saw a splash in the water not far head. Vengeance was one thing; saving Doc was another, and more important. He headed the skiff toward the disturbance in the water, and at the same time slowed the engine, knowing that momentum would carry the skiff the rest of the way.

Tim understood, and appeared to approve. He moved forward as far as he could go, leaning out over the water. More slowly the skiff moved. Now Chuck could see Doc plainly. The boy looked terrified, yet he had stopped swimming, apparently taking a deep breath preparatory to diving again, for in the weak light he probably didn't recognize Tim, whose body was stretched across the bow. Just as Doc was going under, Tim made a grab.

"Got him!" he yelled exultantly.

Then Doc's head and shoulders appeared above the gunwale, as Tim took hold of him with a double grip. Doc looked astonished. Tim struggled with the other's weight. Chuck rose to help him, but Tim called, "Stay back! I can handle him. You might tip us over!"

Tim put forth his strength, and Doc came aboard with a rush, water dripping from his clothing. Tim dragged him to the nearest thwart, and Doc lay there, breathing heavily.

But at last, above the low sputtering of the idling motor, Chuck saw him grin, and heard him say, "Thanks a million! Guess you got here just in time. At first I thought you were Jarvis men who had stolen our boat!"

Doc was all right, Chuck decided. Chuck looked

astern. He could see that the other boat was down almost to its rail, and that the two log pirates were in the water, hanging onto their wreck in order to stay afloat. Probably the wooden skiff wouldn't sink; it was too buoyant for that, even though completely filled. The tug would rescue them. He heard them calling for help.

And on board the tug was activity. The diesel engine began thumping, and Chuck could hear a rattling sound that said the anchor was being raised. Suddenly he remembered Jarvis' rifle.

"Let's get out of here!" he called to Tim. "We've got to get home and fix Doc up with dry clothes."

Tim nodded agreement. "Suits me!" he declared. "Let Jarvis take the rest of the logs, if he wants 'em. Doc comes first!"

Still eying the tug, Chuck glimpsed a brief flash of light. Something went zup! in the air above them; then came the splash of a bullet beyond. As Chuck twisted open the throttle, the thing happened again. This time the bullet struck uncomfortably close. Jarvis was getting the range! It was time to get out of the danger zone.

With the engine firing perfectly, and talking its loudest, the skiff sped away. More bullets came, but they struck astern. With immense relief, Chuck knew that they were safe; now the thing was to get Doc home before the effects of his cold swim brought on possible serious illness.

Nor did they bother just then to question him as to what had happened; there would be plenty of time for that later. He lay shivering on the thwart, yet resting. Kamooks stood close to him, as though the shaggy wolf-dog understood that by so doing he was protecting the boy against the chill wind created by the speed of the boat.

Never had the power skiff moved faster. Yet to Chuck the time seemed to drag until they rounded the last point, and a few minutes later were nosing alongside the float in the lagoon.

11 ... The Closing Trap

*C*lad in dry clothes, yet with his sleeping bag pulled about him, Doc snuggled as close to the crackling open fire as he could get—and still shivered! Clutched in one hand was a hot bowl of canned soup which Tim had prepared, and he ate steadily, as though he needed every bit of the warmth it could give him. Kamooks lay stretched on the floor beside him.

Doc put down the empty soup bowl at last. Some of the pinched blueness had gone out of his features; color had come back into his cheeks. But still he kept the sleeping bag about him, although to Chuck the temperature of the room seemed stifling, for Tim had piled a big arm-load of firewood on the blaze.

"That water wasn't exactly tropical," Doc explained with a wry smile. "Someday, somehow, I hope to get warm again! Maybe I was so scared at first that I didn't notice the cold, but finally I felt it. Plenty!"

They still didn't know how he happened to be in the water, but they let him take his time telling about it. Doc had his own style, and nobody could change it.

"When I saw our boat coming," he went on, "I was sure another pair of log pirates was trying to run me down. Never so glad in all my life that I was mistaken! But I can't understand how you fellows happened to be there."

Chuck explained how they had discovered the beached power skiff, how they had tracked him in the sand and saw where he had approached the cove from the land side.

Doc nodded. "That's right! I spotted the tug standing off the mouth of the cove, and guessed that it had anchored. I took the branding maul and ran for the cove. After I'd been there awhile I saw their skiff leave and head toward shore. Probably they saw me at about the same time, yet the skiff kept coming on. I guess they knew I didn't have a gun, and they weren't afraid of me.

"So," he continued, "I decided to sneak up while they were working on the logs, and start yelling for you fellows as though you were close by and would come help attack 'em. I started out on the raft where they were working, but I made a misstep and fell into the water between two logs." He grimaced at recollection. "Talk about making a fool of myself! The next thing I knew the two pirates had grabbed me, and just so I wouldn't bother them while they were working, they tied my hands and feet with a couple short lengths of rope, and tossed me into their skiff.

"They finished sawing off the ends of six logs," Doc went after a moment, "then started to tow them out of the cove. They didn't know what to do with me, so they took me along in their skiff. When we reached the tug, Lem Jarvis acted like he was crazy.

"He told the men they should have left me behind, but now that I was aboard, he'd finish me off. Said he'd drop me overboard with a chain or some other weight tied to my feet. I'm sure he meant exactly what he said! He sure hates us for getting him into trouble with Stinerson.

"But before they did that, Jarvis said, they'd have to find my boat, smash it up enough so that the weight of the motor would carry it to the bottom. That would wipe out all trace, of myself or the boat. Also, Jarvis said, it would finish the patrol we had set up at the cove.

"Jarvis grinned at me, and said, 'They'll never know what happened, kid. All they can do is guess that maybe some ship ran you down in the night, and sank you!'"

Doc stirred uneasily, at remembrance. "I was scared," he admitted. "All I could do was to pray that they wouldn't find the power skiff, so that they could make an end of things. Unless they found the skiff, they didn't dare kill me because the empty boat might be evidence against them."

He shivered again, whether from the chilling he had suffered, or from sheer terror as he relived the predicament he had been in, it was hard to say. "Just about then," he related, "I discovered that the rope around my wrists had worked loose. They'd left me lying on deck at the stern of the tug. I worked the rope free from my wrists, then untied my feet. Then, when they weren't watching, I took a dive over the rail!

"I stayed underwater as long as I could, and swam hard. When I came up for a fresh breath, I could hear them yelling back there on the tug. Luckily for me, their skiff was some distance away, near shore, searching for our boat. The tug's anchor was down, and the engine wasn't running. Maybe Jarvis didn't think it was necessary to chase me with the tug; their own skiff could do a faster job. But he had to call 'em back, first.

"I saw them coming, and I dived again, swimming underwater until it seemed that my lungs would burst. That was when I began to feel the cold. I felt as though I was swimming among icebergs! But I kept on, heading toward shore, and finally the men in the skiff saw me. They were running me down when you fellows showed up. And, I guess that's about all there is to it!"

Gramps made a harsh sound in his throat. "Blamed murderers!" he growled. "Tim, it was a good job you and Chuck did, in smashin' their skiff. Likely it'll take 'em some time to repair it, or get hold of another, and until that happens, they won't be able to bother the rest of the logs in the cove.

"Too bad them polecats didn't drown! But luck was probably with 'em. Jarvis must have taken 'em aboard. But it didn't prevent him from takin' six more of our logs!" In his anger he grabbed the barrel of the rifle, and thumped the butt of the gun on the floor.

Doc grinned to himself. "In a way," he remarked, "things couldn't have worked out better for us!"

"What's that?" Gramps demanded sharply. "Mean to say that lettin' Jarvis steal our logs is what we want?"

His smile became knowing. "It had to be done," he replied. "In other words, he's walked into our trap!"

"Trap?" The old man's voice was incredulous.

"As Tim has already said," Doc went on, "we've been hoping that some day Lem Jarvis would steal the wrong stick. Well, that's just what he's done!"

"Don't know what you're talkin' about," Gramps declared peevishly.

"Before Jarvis' men reached the cove," Doc explained, "I rebranded every one of those logs. In order to trap Jarvis, it was necessary for him to steal one of those sticks. I've finished my tests, and I think the plan will work!"

"You really mean that?" Chuck asked.

"Play Twenty-Two won't fail!" Doc declared, eyes twinkling with enjoyment.

"Isn't it about time," Chuck persisted, "that you let us in on this big secret of yours?"

Doc shook his head, still relishing the suspense he was creating. "But I'll tell you this much," he conceded, "that we should make another trip to the mainland tomorrow. By that time Jarvis probably will have sold the logs he stole tonight. All we need do is to find which mill bought them. Then I'll undertake to prove that he's a thief!"

"You sound," Tim remarked hopefully, "as though you're sure it can be done!" He glanced at Chuck, as though remembering what the latter had said about Doc's surprising resourcefulness.

"Sometimes the best-laid plans can go wrong," Doc reminded him. Doc yawned. "Man, I'm tired! If nobody has any objections, I'm going to bed!"

The suggestion suited all of them. It seemed unnecessary to maintain the log patrol that night, although the power skiff apparently had been undamaged by the collision. Jarvis probably wouldn't be back until he had a workable small boat to tow the logs out of the cove. They went to bed, and quiet settled over the cabin.

They slept later than usual, and the sun was up three hours when they heard a shrill tooting in the lagoon. A small tug, which neither Chuck nor Doc had seen before, was hove to there, signalling to them.

Tim took a look and declared, "That's Charlie Benson's boat! He tows logs for several of the mills. He's come for our sticks. About time, too! If he'd been here yesterday, we'd have had six more logs for him!"

"But," Doc pointed out, "if he'd towed away those specially marked sticks, we wouldn't have had the trap baited for Jarvis!"

Tim made no reply, yet it was apparent that he was still unconvinced that Doc's plan would work. Six logs meant a lot of money to the Elliotts. They were *real,* whereas Doc's plan was only a theory. Tim went down to the float, talked with the tug's captain, and presently the remaining logs rafted there were taken in tow. Tim came back to the cabin and reported, "They'll pick up the other logs at the cove, also. That cleans us out of timber for the time being. We'll have to knock down some more trees!"

When breakfast was over, and the necessary kitchen work finished, Doc went out to the toolshed where he had been conducting his experiments. He came back carrying a gunny sack, inside which was some medium-sized object.

"What now?" Chuck asked, indicating the sack.

"A present," Doc replied with an enigmatic grin, "for Lem Jarvis. With our compliments, of course!" Then he went down to the float and the waiting power skiff before Chuck could ask further questions. Sometimes, Chuck thought irritably, that guy drives me crazy!

Gramps looked solemn as Tim and Chuck prepared to leave. "You be careful," he warned the boys. "Can't tell what sort of tomfoolishness Doc has in mind, and it could be risky. At the same time, I've got to admit that somehow he's made me feel that our luck is goin' to change. Don't know why; it must be that hope is about the only thing we got left! But, just the same, I don't want you boys to get rambunctious and try tanglin' with Jarvis. There ain't anything that jasper won't do, 'specially to get square with anybody who causes him trouble!"

Tim nodded. "We'll be careful, Gramps," he promised. "And you can be sure we won't start anything we can't finish!"

"Good luck, then!" the old man said.

Kamooks went with the boys as far as the door, but stopped there when Tim commanded him to stay. They wouldn't need Kamooks this trip.

Once more the vast sweep of Puget Sound seemed so calm and peaceful that it was hard to realize it had ever known destructive storms or man-made violence. Doc, with his mysterious sack lying on the floorboards just in front of him, just to make certain that Chuck and Tim didn't get too curious about what it contained, took his usual place at the engine, and soon the power skiff was racing out of the lagoon, bound on its unusual quest.

Tim leaned over and said to Chuck, "I told Benson to take our logs to Stinerson's mill. Can't forget how Stinerson backed us up in that row with Jarvis. He may run short of logs, now that he has stopped buying from Jarvis."

Chuck nodded, deciding that Tim's gratitude and thoughtfulness were good qualities, and a clue to the honest nature of this Skookum-Chuck boy.

"So," Tim went on, "there's no use wasting time by going to Stinerson's mill again in search of these stolen logs. Jarvis has sold them to one of his other markets. It may take us some time to find out what he did with them. First we'll try Mike Flood. He has a small mill south of Stinerson's a few miles."

He waved back to Doc, indicating the course they were to take. The power skiff hurried onward. Before long it came to rest alongside the booms surrounding the log pond of a mill neither Chuck nor Doc had visited before.

Mike Flood obviously knew Tim, and was curious when the boy told him that they were looking for logs which Jarvis had sold that day.

"None here," Flood answered. "Haven't seen Jarvis for a week. What's all this about, Tim? I heard that Ole Stinerson had a run-in with Jarvis, and that Stinerson is hinting around that maybe Jarvis isn't on the square with his log dealings. Anything to it?"

"That's what we're trying to prove," Tim explained. "Well, Mr. Flood, if you don't have any Jarvis logs, we'll keep on looking."

At Tim's directions, the power skiff moved along the shore until another mill was reached. Once more Tim made the inquiry, and once more he received substantially the same answer. As they started off again, Chuck asked doubtfully, "Is it possible that Jarvis hasn't sold the logs so far, but is hiding them somewhere until he finds out what we are doing?"

Tim shook his head emphatically. "I don't think so," he replied. "There seems no reason why he should want to wait. Probably he isn't worried about us at all; besides he *has* to get rid of the logs in a hurry. He wouldn't have any place to keep them, unless he found some little-known cove on one of the outer islands. Towing them there would take time. He—"

Tim broke off, staring ahead. "There's Jarvis' tug now!" he cried excitedly. "Tied up at Pete Dawson's mill. *That's* where we're going to find our logs!"

Chuck also looked ahead. A quarter-mile distant he saw that another small mill was nestled in an indentation in the coastline. There was the usual log pond, and beside it was the pirate tug, moored to the outer boomsticks.

"They have the boom open," Tim went on, his voice rising, "and are poking logs inside it. We got here just in time!"

He swung around toward Doc, and made chopping motions with his hands as a signal to slow the motor. Doc obeyed, and the speed of the skiff fell away.

Chuck guessed that Jarvis and his men were probably so busy delivering the stolen logs that as yet they hadn't observed the power skiff approaching. Maybe Jarvis didn't care; there seemed to be no reason why he should worry. The stolen logs already carried his own brand; that made them his legal property. Tim Elliott's trick of stamping the HE brand into the bark hadn't worked.

Yet Chuck had a grim feeling of satisfaction as he saw that the skiff which he and Tim had smashed was now carried on the tug's afterdeck. Even from that distance it appeared to be twisted and badly damaged.

Doc eased the power skiff alongside the boom, a hundred yards from the tug. Nobody on the latter craft appeared to notice. Then Tim led the way, with Chuck following and Doc, carrying the laden gunny sack and bringing up the rear, toward an elderly man who stood talking with the tall log pirate. For the first time, then, the tug's crew helping the boom-men handle the logs saw the boys, and the men stopped work momentarily.

Jarvis eyed the three boys in malevolent silence as they came up, and Tim said, "Good morning, Mr. Dawson! Been buying some more logs?"

Dawson, a gray-haired, rather kindly-looking man, seemed surprised at the question. "Hello, Tim!" he returned the greeting. Then, "Why, yes, I've just bought a half-dozen sticks from Lem Jarvis, here."

Tim nodded. "Mind if I look them over?" he asked the mill owner.

The latter seemed even more surprised. "Of course not!" he agreed affably. "But why such interest? Anything wrong, Tim?"

"Maybe," Tim replied. "That's why we're here—to find out!"

Jarvis glowered. "I know what's up," he told the mill owner. "Dawson, don't let these kids try to fool you! They tried to put over a whizzer on me at Stinerson's mill. Nearly got away with it, too! This here Tim Elliott had gone and stomped his brand onto my sticks, then tried to make Stinerson believe that he'd done it at the time he cut the logs himself. Boldest thing I ever saw!

"Of course," he added venomously, "I exposed his trick. He'd sneaked up to one of my rafts durin' the night, I reckon, and marked the sticks, then claimed 'em as his own!"

Dawson said nothing, but his manner, as he eyed Tim, seemed almost accusing.

"It's an outrage!" Jarvis went on, his voice hurt

174

and angry. "A dirty trick, and I won't stand for such a thing! If it happens again, I'll see what the law can do to protect a man's reputation!"

Dawson appeared impressed, and yet obviously he did not fully share Jarvis' indignation. "What about it, Tim?" he asked quietly.

Tim took a deep breath. "I'm not going to argue with Lem Jarvis," he told Dawson. "All I'm asking for at this time is your permission to look at these logs he sold you. Even if they have my brand stamped into the bark, I won't ask you to believe that they're mine. But maybe I can *prove* that he stole them last night!"

Dawson's brows drew together. "You can?" he asked in astonishment. "How?"

"Will you let me *try,* Mr. Dawson? Maybe that's the best way to answer your question!"

Dawson shrugged. "Sounds fair enough," he admitted. "How do you want to go about it?"

"Listen, Dawson!" Jarvis broke in, a trace of uneasiness in his voice. "You think I'm goin' to stand here and let this kid call me a log thief? What sort of a man do you think I am?"

Dawson's eyes twinkled for an instant, then became cold. "I'm not too sure about that myself, Lem," he retorted. "All I'm trying to do is to be fair. It seems odd to me that Tim Elliott would come here and accuse you of stealing his logs unless he had some way of proving what he was saying. Why not have the matter cleared up, here and now?"

Jarvis tried to appear generous. "Suits me!" he declared confidently. "But," he added warningly, "if he's tryin' again to put over that cock-and-bull story about stompin' his brand onto my logs, then I'm goin' to take action!"

"That's your privilege, Lem," Dawson said. "Well, Tim, what do you want me to do?"

The boy turned to Doc. "I guess," he said doubtfully, "that this is where you start carrying the ball!"

Tim was plainly very nervous. His face was pale despite its coating of deep tan. It was plain that he didn't know what was going to happen, and that he was tremendously worried over the outcome. He was putting all his faith in Doc Peters, realizing that failure now meant total defeat. If Doc failed, it meant triumph for Lem Jarvis, a would-be killer, a cunning and dangerous enemy.

These thoughts raced through Chuck's mind as he watched the setting of the scene. He understood the uneasiness which Tim felt, and, for that matter, he was also deeply worried.

Yet Doc seemed amazingly confident. He had belief in himself. And that belief must have been contagious, for Chuck suddenly found new hope as he heard Doc say matter-of-factly, "Thanks, Tim!" Then to the mill owner, he said, "Mr. Dawson, will you please have one of the Jarvis logs brought here and lifted clear of the water?"

"You'll find nothin' but the LJ brand!" Jarvis declared vehemently.

Doc ignored him. "Will *that* be too much trouble, Mr. Dawson?" he asked pleasantly.

The man shrugged. "I suppose not," he agreed. His

voice sounded patient, yet it was obvious to Chuck that Dawson considered the request somewhat childish. Nevertheless, his curiosity had been aroused. Possibly, too, the situation had aroused honest doubt in his mind that Lem Jarvis was as innocent as he pretended to be. Dawson often bought logs from Jarvis. If there was anything wrong, he wanted to know about it as soon as possible.

He called to the nearest boom-man, and told the latter to work one of the Jarvis logs up to the moving chain which carried sticks up to the saw carriage. In a few minutes the thing had been accomplished.

"Put it on the chain," Dawson directed. "We'll stop it halfway up the slip."

This was done. As soon as the stick was halfway up the slope, Dawson yelled to a man who apparently operated the lever controlling the log chain, for with a clanking noise, the chain stopped abruptly. The stick rested clear in the log slip.

"Thanks, Mr. Dawson!" said Doc. It seemed to Chuck that the mill owner was certainly going all-out in the matter of cooperating, for he had momentarily shut down his plant. Until the log chain started moving again, no timber could reach the saws, and most of the crew would be idle.

As though understanding what this work stoppage meant, Doc announced, "I'll make it as fast as I can!"

Reaching inside the gunny sack he pulled out what Chuck had already suspected was there—the blowtorch—although Chuck still didn't know what Doc intended to do. Quickly, Doc pumped more air into the torch by means of the piston built into the brass chamber, then opened the feed valve a little until a few drops of gasoline oozed into an iron cup below the burner. He struck a match and lit this liquid fuel. The fire covered the burner. He waited perhaps a half-minute, then opened the feed valve again, thus releasing air pressure which made a hissing noise and sent a spear of bluish flame shooting out from the mouth of the burner tube. As the burner grew hotter, Doc opened the feed valve more until the torch began to roar at full power.

In a half-ring behind him, the others watched with intense interest as though this simple matter of lighting a blowtorch was some wondrous thing they had never seen before. Presently Doc seemed satisfied with the way the torch was working, for he lifted it by means of its handle, and stepped to the upper end of the waiting log. The others followed him, still gripped by curiosity.

Chuck saw what he had expected—that the log-end had several LJ marks from Jarvis' branding maul. But Doc avoided these. Instead, he let the flame from the torch play over unmarked portions of the wood, which began to blacken at once. Very slowly he moved the flame over the surface, as though seeking something. The acrid smell of the charring wood filled the air.

Suddenly his face split in a grin. Deftly, now, he eased the torch backward until only the tip of the fire tongue licked against the end of the log. For a few seconds he held the flame there; then stood up and faced Dawson.

"Take a look, will you?" he suggested quietly.

Dawson stepped forward, and bent down for a closer examination. So, too, did the others, including Lem Jarvis. And suddenly Chuck felt like yelling with delight; he fought down an impulse to throw his arms around Doc Peters and hug him. Doc's latest Play Twenty-Two had worked!

Faintly outlined in the blackened wood—brought back to life by the heat of the blowtorch—was the familiar HE brand of the Elliotts of Skookum-Chuck Island!

12 ... The Unexpected

For a long moment nothing was said; all of them seemed astounded at what they had seen. It was Pete Dawson who finally spoke.

"Tim Elliott is right!" he declared. "That log belongs to him. And so do the others. I'll bet that blowtorch will bring out the HE brand on *all* of them!"

He swung around to Jarvis. "Well," he demanded, "what have you to say? Better talk fast, mister!"

Jarvis, confused, found voice. "It's a blasted trick!" he cried. "I don't know how he did it, but it just ain't true!"

"It's true enough," Doc asserted. "When Tim, here, hit the log hard with his branding maul, he jarred the wood fibers back for several inches, packing them tightly. The heat from the torch caused them to expand; that's what made the injured fibers stand out against the rest of the wood. Got the idea out of a textbook on cellulose. Trouble is, Mr. Jarvis," he went on with exaggerated politeness, "the cookies you sawed off Tim's logs weren't thick. Maybe if you'd cut at least a foot of wood off each end, the torch wouldn't have brought out the brandmark!"

"Lot of silly nonsense!" Jarvis insisted. But Dawson took issue with him.

"It's not nonsense, Jarvis, and you know it!" he declared. "It's the kind of evidence that will stand up in any court."

"You got nothin' on me!" Jarvis retorted. He reached into his Mackinaw pocket and pulled out a slip of paper. "Your check, see? I'm tearin' it up!" He ripped the thing into shreds. "The deal for them logs is off! Now, try provin' anything against me!"

Dawson laughed mirthlessly. "It will be easy enough. My men are witnesses that you sold those logs to me. The boys and myself saw how the HE brand was brought out on a log which already carried your brand!"

"I'm takin' them logs back," Jarvis announced. "You got no right to stop me!"

"That's what you think!" Dawson declared. He called over to his boom-men. "Stand by with your pike poles, boys! If Jarvis tries to take away any of those logs he just delivered, you know what to do!" The boom-men looked puzzled, not understanding what was going on, yet they understood the order, for they began moving toward the other Jarvis logs at the outer boom. Jarvis' men made no attempt to stop them.

The man apparently saw that he was defeated. Muttering, he started off toward his tug.

"Let him go!" Dawson directed the boom-men. To the boys, he said, "He won't get away. I'm going to phone the sheriff, and swear out a warrant charging Lem Jarvis with grand larceny. He tried to make me a party to a crooked deal. I've suspected for a long time that he was a log thief, but there was no way of proving it—and I needed logs to keep my mill running. But I'm not going to have people think that I'm dealing in stolen timber."

To Tim he said, "Those six logs I bought from Jarvis are yours; I'm sure of it. But I can't buy them from you until his case is settled in court. You can leave them here with me, and I won't make them into lumber until this affair is ended. I paid him three hundred and eighty-nine dollars for them, according to my own scale. Is that price satisfactory, Tim?"

The boy grinned. "Swell, Mr. Dawson! I know that Gramps is going to be tickled over the way things have turned out!"

The mill owner smiled. Then he turned and patted Doc Peters on the shoulder. "That was a great trick," he approved. "Best I've ever seen! Maybe as a result of it all log pirates on Puget Sound will be afraid to keep on."

Doc flushed at the praise. "It wasn't my idea," he explained. "I got it out of a book," he repeated.

"Tim and his grandfather ought to be thankful that you did," Dawson remarked.

"We couldn't be more so!" Tim declared fervently. Chuck reached out and grabbed Doc's hand. "Good job, fella!" he said feelingly. Doc nodded, then swallowed hard, as though he did not dare trust himself to speak. It was plain that reaction from the ordeal had hit him just as hard as it had the others. For once Doc, instead of affecting boastfulness, seemed humble. Chuck was immensely proud of him.

Dawson returned to the mill, obviously determined to notify the sheriff of what had happened. Jarvis' tug was already underway, heading seaward toward the outer islands. As the three boys embarked again in the power skiff, bound homeward, Chuck wondered where Jarvis was going, what he was going to do.

Would he escape? Dawson had said confidently that he wouldn't get away. But the sweep of Puget Sound is great, and there were many places where Jarvis and his tug could hole-up, at least for a time. The Canadian border was only a few hours' run northward; maybe Jarvis could find sanctuary there, hoping that pursuit would ease up. Or he might even go on to Alaska. Chuck wasn't sure that the authorities would take the trouble to follow him there.

Some intuition told Chuck that they hadn't seen the last of Lem Jarvis. He was a vengeful man, as Gramps had said. His illicit career as a Puget Sound log pirate had been ended. Would he be content to let that happen without trying to take revenge?

But no matter how uneasy Chuck felt, he decided there was no use bothering Tim and Doc with his thoughts. It was enough to realize that there would be no more logs stolen from Skookum-Chuck Island. Gramps and Tim could carry out their plans without further trouble. This should be a moment of victory, not worry.

Yet it was evident that Tim was also deep in thought. Restless, too, for he shifted about on the thwart, looking in all directions. By now, Jarvis' tug was vanishing around a point of the nearest island. Tim stared after it, then turned and called back to Doc, "Can you make better speed? The tide is running against us, and if we don't hurry we'll be a long time getting home!"

Chuck wondered at Tim's impatience. Of course, it was understandable that Tim wanted to get back to Skookum-Chuck and Gramps with the news as quickly as possible, yet ordinarily he wasn't in a great hurry about anything. He seemed to know what he wanted to do, and he did it without any fussing.

Doc nodded, and tinkered with the carburetor; then he twisted the throttle open wider, and the skiff gained speed. The engine was delivering full power, and the boat seemed to be tearing along, but Tim obviously was not satisfied. Still, apparently realizing that they couldn't go faster, he kept silent, facing ahead.

Chuck guessed that Tim was worrying about Lem Jarvis. At the moment Gramps was alone on the island, save for what protection Kamooks could give him. Tim wanted to get home as quickly as possible to make certain that his grandfather was safe.

The sturdy little outboard motor was doing its best, but the tide, as Tim had remarked, was running strongly in the opposite direction. They made progress, but slowly. There was no telling where Jarvis' tug had gone. Maybe it had continued northward— or it might now be hiding among the islands.

What were the authorities doing? How would they go about rounding up the log pirate gang?

Tim spoke suddenly. "There's Bill Fuller's log patrol tug," he told Chuck. "It's coming from the mainland. It has plenty of power, and should pass us before we get home."

Tim looked longingly in the direction of Skookum-Chuck. "We ought not to delay ourselves," he went on, "but I'd really like to tell Fuller what happened at Dawson's mill."

"Maybe we won't have to lose any time," Chuck suggested. "If the tug holds its course it should pass close to us before we reach home. If it doesn't overtake us, or if it changes course, we can cut over and head it off."

Tim nodded as though the plan suited him. The power skiff kept on bucking the swift-running tidal currents which, Chuck had heard, sometimes reach a velocity of eight miles an hour in the narrow waterways between the many islands.

Skookum-Chuck loomed larger. Jarvis' tug was still out of sight. Then they observed that Fuller's log patrol craft was veering away toward the north.

Tim signalled to Doc to change course accordingly. "We'll have to stop long enough to speak to Fuller," he decided. "It might be important—especially if he doesn't know that Jarvis is trying to get away!"

The power skiff swung around in a right-angled

turn, and now it began to make better time as it quartered the tide instead of fighting straight against it. Apparently Fuller saw them at last, and guessed what they wanted to do, for his tug slowed. They came alongside, and he called down, "I'm in a hurry, Tim! What's on your mind?"

The boy started to explain what had happened, but Fuller, with a wave of his hand, cut him short.

"Already heard about it," he said. "I was on my way home when they called me on the radiophone. I turned back, and I'm trying to help them overhaul Jarvis right now. The sheriff has already flashed word to his deputies on most of the islands. Even the Coast Guard has been alerted. We'll have Jarvis and his gang rounded up before dark!"

Chuck felt relief. Tim's grin said that *he* felt the same way! Pete Dawson had really started the law wheels turning, just as he had promised. With the hunt for Jarvis already on, it wasn't likely that they would have to worry about him further. They waved acknowledgment to Fuller, and once more they were homeward-bound.

Gramps' seamed faced lighted up when they told him what had happened at Dawson's mill. Kamooks wagged his tail briskly as though he understood every word they were saying. When the story was done, Chuck saw unmistakable tears glistening on the cheeks of the old man. A lump came into Chuck's throat, and he turned away abruptly, as though afraid to show his own feelings.

Then Gramps said, "Come here, youngsters!" He

took their hands in both of his, and seemed to be fighting down the emotion which stirred him. "Never felt so good in my life!" he declared huskily. "Tim, I reckon we didn't realize our luck when Chuck and Doc were driven ashore on Skookum-Chuck by that storm. But that's the way it usually goes; folks don't recognize good luck the first time they see it!"

He took a deep breath, striving to get hold of himself. "Well, now, Tim," he went on, "it seems like you're goin' to have your chance after all! You've got the rest of the summer to put up enough logs to pay for your schoolin' and then some. I'd like right well for you to go to the same school as they do," and he indicated the other boys, "because I figure you'll be happier there. Play football or any other fool game you like! Enjoy a little of the fun you've missed all these years!

"Don't you worry about me while you're away," he concluded. "We'll have old Luke Peterson come over here, same as before, and look after things. Him and me—we get along fine!"

Somewhat unsteadily, Tim replied, "Thanks, Gramps! It sounds wonderful." He looked as though he wanted to say more, but didn't dare trust himself to speak. Chuck understood how the Skookum-Chuck boy must feel. He'd lived a lonely life, with hard work and few pleasures. Now the situation had been miraculously changed. This was a moment when the unsaid thought went deeper than words.

As though to cover his confusion, Tim suggested, "There's still a good part of the day left. Let's cut some more logs! To me it will seem fun, now that I know they're not going to be stolen!"

Doc cleared his throat impressively. "Gentlemen," he announced, "I'm available! You fellows have been having all the fun, knocking over trees and shooting 'em down that hill, while I've been slaving my life away over a hot blowtorch!"

Chuck thought wryly, Here we go again! He's back in the old groove! Yet nothing Doc could say hereafter would be really annoying. He'd already proved that behind his consistent clowning he was downright sincere and capable. Doc was okay!

Kamooks was left behind with Gramps. As Tim had remarked, the logging job now seemed like fun. Doc insisted on handling one end of the falling-saw, and Chuck took quiet delight in bossing him and explaining how the work should be done. Letting the pair work things out together, Tim readied the choker and with his axe swamped away the brush along a strip where the tree would fall. He also did most of the work of chopping out the notch. When the forest giant crashed to earth at last, Doc seemed as pleased as though he had just run back a punt for a touchdown.

"Man!" he exclaimed admiringly. "This is really living! Who'd ever thought I could flatten a big tree like that?"

Tim grinned at his enthusiasm. "You had a little help," he pointed out, nodding his head toward Chuck.

"So I did!" Doc admitted, mock surprise in his

voice. "But not much," he added thoughtfully. Chuck picked up a clod of earth and threw it at him.

They cut three trees, trimmed off the limbs, and sent the long sticks downward. Then Tim announced that they had done enough for the day, and that by the time the sticks were bucked into logs, it would be nightfall. Yet Doc, apparently still reveling in his new-found ability to help send a mighty fir thundering to the ground, insisted on cutting just one more tree. "That will mean three or four more logs for you," he argued with Tim. "Maybe tomorrow I won't feel like logging at all. Better let me work while I'm in the mood for it!"

Tim could scarcely refuse the request; besides, he, too, was anxious to produce as many logs as possible. Chuck told Doc warningly, "All right, Paul Bunyan! But I'll bet your muscles will be so sore tomorrow morning that you can't even roll out of bed. That's the way *I* felt after the first day on this job!"

They made short work of the fourth tree, a big one. Because the hour was late, Tim merely anchored the stick to a stump by means of the choker, lopped off the limbs, and said they would wait until tomorrow before sending it into the water. "We've still got three sticks to buck into logs, as it is," he pointed out.

The tremendous spar lay stretched on the ground, its ponderous weight pulling so tightly on the choker that the latter was like a stiff steel rod. Tim looked it over and decided, "She'll hold until morning. Then, all we have to do is knock out the clevis pin, and away she'll go. Hope that choker doesn't slip. These sticks land pretty close to the float, and I'd hate to be down there when a wild one came down the hill!"

Night had arrived by the time they had finished bucking up the last stick already in the water. They saw with satisfaction that their work had produced ten fine logs. These were branded, then rafted together and moored to the float. The weather was calm. The raft would be safe until next morning, when they'd use the power skiff to tow it to the cove.

Dinner was almost like a holiday celebration, with talk, laughter, and banter on Doc's part. Yet before long they were willing to go to bed, for it had been a tiring as well as an exciting day. Just before Chuck dropped off in slumber, his thoughts went back to Lem Jarvis.

But not for long. Even log pirates couldn't keep him awake. He closed his eyes, and the next thing he knew it was morning.

Already there was the tempting, blended aroma of freshly made coffee and frying bacon in the cabin. Chuck looked over at Doc, and saw that the latter was still sleeping. Chuck grabbed his shoulder, and shook him. "Get up! Breakfast's ready!"

Doc stirred, then groaned. "What was the final score?" he asked weakly.

"Score?"

"They must have made a dozen touchdowns. Their whole team kept running over me!"

Chuck laughed. "So, the brawny muscle-man had to keep on knocking down trees until he got himself a flock of Charley horses!" He made a jeering noise. "Wake up, logger! It's daylight in the swamp, and we're going to cut a lot more sticks as soon as breakfast is over!"

Doc shuddered. "Not me! I'll be in bed for a week!"

"Okay, sissy!" Chuck went out.

Gramps greeted him breezily. Tim was in the kitchen, busy preparing food. "Doc won't be of much help to us today," Chuck reported, and told him what had happened.

Tim chuckled. "I guessed he was overdoing it. Well, we won't need him. We'll tow that raft to the cove first, then come back and slide that last stick into the water." His face sobered. "Wonder if they've caught Lem Jarvis yet," he added, as though thinking aloud.

"Maybe we'll know soon," Chuck replied. "Anyway, I can't see that it matters much. He's done for, in these parts. If he hasn't already been captured, then he's probably running away as fast as he can!"

"I suppose so," Tim agreed. "Still—"

He broke off as a drawn-out hooting from a tugboat reached them. "That's Bill Fuller's boat!" he exclaimed. Both boys rushed out of the cabin.

They saw the log patrol craft hove to in deep water out beyond the float, and Fuller was leaning out of the wheelhouse window. They hurried down to the shore, waving to him.

"Thought I'd drop by and tell you that Jarvis' tug and four-man crew were picked up late yesterday," he announced. "Sheriff Dunham's men turned Jarvis back just before he reached the Canadian line. The sheriff's posse had borrowed one of our log patrol boats in order to hunt for him. Jarvis' tug and crew were taken to Anacortes. The men are in jail!"

Both boys brightened at the news. But Fuller didn't seem too enthusiastic. "Only one thing spoils the picture," he went on. "Jarvis got away!"

"G-got away?" Tim stuttered.

Fuller nodded. "Our boat, with the sheriff's men aboard, was herding Jarvis' tug back home," he explained, "when they passed close to Shaw Island. Jarvis slipped over the side and swam ashore before they could stop him. They combed the island for him, but he managed to stay hidden. Then this morning they found that during the night he'd stolen a small boat and rowed off. There's been no trace of him since.

"Of course, they'll get him! He can't hide out among these islands for long." He added, "I knew you folks would like to know the situation. Seems to me there isn't a chance in a million that he'll show up on Skookum-Chuck. This is one place he'll likely stay away from! But it won't do any harm to keep your eyes peeled."

A bell clanged deep inside the tug as Fuller signalled his engineer. "Got to be mooching along!" he told the boys. He waved to them, and then the log patrol craft began heading outward.

For a long moment the boys stood there in silence. Still in silence they turned and made their way to the cabin. Just before they reached it, Tim remarked,

"This is surely going to disappoint Gramps! Yet I think Fuller is right—Jarvis won't dare show up *here!* Isn't that the way you see it, Chuck?" Tim's voice sounded almost pleading.

Chuck replied rather evasively, "It seems to make sense for Jarvis to stay away from a place where he's known. And it's certain, too, that they'll nab him soon." Tim nodded, as though he found comfort in the other's words.

Gramps pounded the arm of his chair angrily when he heard the news. "So, the law men messed it up!" he exclaimed. "Sure, they got most of those high-binders, but Lem Jarvis is the key man!" He reached over and took hold of the gun, sliding his right hand up and down the barrel. "If he shows up here," Gramps declared ominously, "they won't have to do any more huntin' for him!"

Tim and Chuck said nothing. Chuck took another look at Doc. He was sound asleep once more! Well, there'd be plenty of time later to tell him what had happened. Chuck rejoined Tim in the living room, and then they went down to the float. The previous day's cut of logs had to be towed to the cove.

Ten such sticks, they soon discovered, made a heavy drag for the power skiff, particularly so because the tide was wrong. Chuck handled the engine, and the skiff and its tow moved slowly along the shore. The loud exhaust of the outboard motor made conversation difficult, and they didn't attempt it; probably neither boy felt much like talking, anyway. Chuck scanned the empty seascape, thinking, At least we don't have to worry about meeting Jarvis' tug! There was that much comfort in the situation.

It took time to make the trip, but at last they turned into the entrance of the cove. There were no logs rafted there now, for the last of them had been towed to Stinerson's mill, as Tim had directed. Carefully, Chuck guided skiff and tow past the water-worn rocks, and toward the empty booms. He waited for Tim to signal him when to slow the engine.

They were still a hundred yards from the boom-sticks when the thing happened. Tim faced about suddenly, gesturing, and Chuck throttled down. Then Tim was pointing toward shore, an anxious expression on his face. Chuck's gaze followed the direction the other had indicated.

Drawn up on the beach was a small skiff!

Chuck knew he had never seen the craft before. The thought occurred to him that it might belong to some islander who had merely landed in the cove to wait for a change of tide before resuming the long pull to the mainland.

Yet second thought told him that this wasn't the case at all. He recalled what Fuller had said about the manner of Jarvis' escape and flight from Shaw Island; of the stolen rowboat. There could be only one reasonable explanation of the presence of this strange skiff here.

Lem Jarvis had landed on Skookum-Chuck!

13 ... Reckoning

*N*either boy spoke at once. It wasn't necessary.

Chuck stared at the deserted shore, and the woods beyond. Nothing moved, so far as he could see. Yet surely Lem Jarvis was on the island, perhaps in hiding and watching them at this very moment.

He must be unarmed; he could scarcely have taken his rifle along when he escaped from the tug by swimming to Shaw Island. That was one comforting thought. If he had a gun, they would be easy targets out here in the center of this small cove.

Tim reacted quickly. He slid aft, keeping his voice low so that it would not carry to shore and let Jarvis hear what he was saying. "Got to work fast!" he exclaimed. "We'll let the logs go; they won't drift out of the cove. Even if they do, it doesn't matter. We've got to get back to the cabin, and put Gramps and Doc on guard!"

Swiftly he untied the towline, tossed it overboard.

"Wind up that motor," he told Chuck, "and let's get out of here in a hurry!"

Chuck obeyed. As the power skiff swung around and headed out of the cove he had a moment of uneasiness. After all, they couldn't be *sure* that Jarvis didn't have a gun! It wouldn't have surprised Chuck too much to hear bullets ripping through the air. Imagination, of course, but he couldn't help it. Yet in a matter of seconds he knew that it wasn't going to happen, for the skiff had passed through the entrance and was turning homeward.

Tim, face drawn with worry, sat there stiffly, staring ahead, as though trying by mental concentration to make the boat go faster. But the power skiff was already doing its best, and now the tide was favoring it. The rugged shoreline seemed to race past. In a matter of minutes they glimpsed the familiar point of land which marked the lagoon, and home.

With the motor still roaring wide open, they shot toward the float, and only at the last second before they were dangerously close did Chuck close the throttle and let momentum carry them onward.

Their eyes went first to the cabin, but everything seemed peaceful there. Smoke rose from the chimney as usual. The skiff bumped the float, and Tim leaped out and made the boat fast. Just as he did so, both boys were startled by the crashing report of a rifle which came from the cabin.

Chuck felt his heart jump into his throat. Again came a shot. Then they heard the muffled voice of Kamooks.

"Gramps!" Tim cried. "Come on!" An instant later both of them were pounding up the slight rise to the cabin. Without hesitating, Tim flung open the door.

Doc stood there wide-eyed, in the center of the room, one hand gripping the collar of the wolf-dog, who was frantically trying to break away. Gramps sat at the window, his body twisted half around as he peered outside. The window sash was up a few inches, and the barrel of his old rifle was poked through this opening. As they entered, they saw him squinting along the barrel. He pulled the trigger, and the gun butt jerked against his shoulder. Once more the weapon spoke loudly.

"Gramps!" Tim shouted.

The old man turned, his features working. "Jarvis is out yonder!" he announced. "Just saw him." He worked the lever of the repeater, pumping another cartridge into the chamber.

"Spotted him sneakin' down the trail toward us," Gramps went on. "Wasn't more than a hundred yards off, then. Reckon he saw me at the same time, because he ducked into the brush and started runnin'. I cut loose with the gun, but missed him. He's still up there!"

"Kamooks tried to get out," Doc explained hurriedly. "He must have seen or smelled Jarvis. But Gramps made me keep him inside."

"Jarvis might kill him," Gramps pointed out. "Anyway, I wouldn't dare shoot if Kamooks was up there in the brush, too!"

Tim turned to Doc. "We've got to get word to the

sheriff—fast!" he decided. "You can make that skiff do its best. Get to the mainland!"

"And leave you fellows here to fight this out?" Doc protested.

"It's the only way," Tim assured him. "We'll handle things here. We saw Jarvis' rowboat in the cove; maybe we've scared him so that he'll go back to it and try to reach some other island. But if the sheriff knows that Jarvis has been here, it will narrow the hunt. Understand? You've got an important job to do!"

"Okay, then." Doc went out of the cabin and ran down to the float. Soon they heard the roar of the outboard motor, and saw the power skiff racing out of the lagoon.

Gramps kept watch at the window. "Never shot at a man before," he confessed, "but I reckon I've got no choice now. Lem Jarvis is a killer. He's come to Skookum-Chuck to wipe us out, if he can!"

"No more shooting, Gramps!" Tim said firmly. "Jarvis can't be armed, and now that we're on guard, he can't do much to hurt us!"

"He could set the island afire!" Gramps insisted.

Tim hesitated. The suggestion was alarming to Chuck. Yet Tim shook his head positively.

"No," he declared, "Jarvis won't try *that!* There's no wind; besides, the underbrush is still damp from the last rain. It won't work, and he knows it!"

Gramps said, "Guess you're right," and kept peering out of the window. Suddenly he bent his head, and squinted along the gun barrel.

"No!" Tim cried. He reached over and seized the rifle.

"But," Gramps protested, "I just glimpsed him yonder! Up on the hill side, where you've been cuttin' trees. I tell you, he's up to somethin'! If I could drop a bullet close to him, he'd likely skedaddle!"

Tim likewise stared out of the window. "He's there, all right," Tim decided. "But what could he be doing? If he was smart, he'd have gone over the hill to the cove where he left his boat."

Chuck remarked wonderingly, "He seems to be fooling around with that big stick we left up there yesterday!"

Suddenly Tim gave an exclamation of disbelief and alarm. "No!" he cried.

"What say?" Gramps demanded.

"He's working on that stick which we anchored with the choker!" Tim reported. "He's using a pole to move the lower end of it sideways along the hill!"

"What for?"

Tim's voice became shrill with excitement and apprehension. "Maybe he's trying to point the stick this way—right at the cabin! The way we left the stick yesterday, it was aimed at the water near the float. But if he can change the angle of it, it could come straight at us! He's crazy!"

He swung around to Chuck. "We've got to stop him!" Tim declared. "Come on!"

"Wait!" begged Gramps. "I'll stop him with a bullet!"

"No!" Tim ordered. "The range is too far. You

couldn't scare him off if you shot at him all day. There isn't time to try it!"

He added hurriedly, "Keep Kamooks with you, Gramps! Wait until we get up there; then let him go. We'll leave the door open. If the dog gets there ahead of us, Jarvis will kill him. But he can come up and help us when the scrap starts!"

"Take this gun!" Gramps urged. But Tim was already out of the place, Chuck behind him, leaving the door ajar. They could hear Kamooks raging to follow them, but Gramps evidently had a firm grip on the dog's collar.

They went fast, following the trail which they had used before to reach the woods operation. It was a steep trail, yet Tim ran on almost as rapidly as though the ground was level. Chuck managed to keep pace, grateful for the fact that he was in good condition although the football season had ended many months before. Yet before long he found himself breathing heavily, while Tim seemed strung with rawhide and steel wires.

Soon they were halfway up the slope, and still running. Jarvis was in plain sight, and it was apparent that he was doing the very thing Tim had guessed: he had a pole and he was struggling with the tapering end of the downed tree, swinging it inch by inch in the direction of the cabin below. Because the tip was the lighter end of the long spar, and springy, he was working it around. Even from this distance, Chuck could see that the man had moved the stick several feet. When he had shifted it a little more, he could

knock out the clevis pin, and the giant javelin would shoot downward, to wreak destruction on the cabin or anything else in its path. Jarvis must be insane!

Down below, Gramps must be watching. Probably he was praying, too, as he understood this battle against time. For he was crippled, helpless.

Jarvis paused in his grim work, and looked up. He straightened—and Chuck knew that for the first time Jarvis was aware that the two boys were coming up the slope. He took only a brief glimpse; then attacked his job more furiously than ever.

The stick had moved a couple more feet as the boys neared. Jarvis knew he was rushed for time; he couldn't make certain that he had the stick aimed as he wanted it. He dropped the pole, picked up a stone as big as his fist, and leaped toward the choker and began pounding on the clevis pin.

There was a metallic click, and the pin fell half out. But the choker still held. Jarvis yelled disappointment, turned, and hurled the stone straight at Tim, only a few feet away, and charged at him.

There was no time for Tim to dodge. The missile struck him full in the chest, and he gave a startled "Ugh!" and fell. Chuck, leaping over him, leaned forward and dived at Jarvis.

It was a terrific shoulder block, and it hit the man just above the knees, and sent him sprawling backward. Lem Jarvis probably had never played football in his life, and this battering-ram jolt was a maneuver new to him. Yet he was a powerful man, and he outweighed Chuck by at least fifty pounds. He rolled over, got up, and started toward the boy, swinging big fists. But before one of his blows could connect, he was knocked off his feet again.

Then Chuck was aware that Tim was up, and boring in. "Block him!" Chuck cried, for he saw that Tim, fists doubled, was courageously attempting to trade blows with the man who towered over him. Yet whether Tim understood, or whether he did not know how to block, was not clear.

He did succeed in ducking one of Jarvis' swings, and countered with a hard punch to the man's middle. Yet the next instant Jarvis' fist caught Tim on the shoulder and sent him spinning backward. Before Jarvis could recover, Chuck smashed him with another shoulder block.

The man yelled as he went down. He seemed unable to understand this sort of fighting.

Yet Chuck's triumph was brief. Jarvis twisted quickly, and half crawled, half ran toward the jammed clevis. He seized another rock, and battered the mechanism. Then Chuck, preparing to rush him again, barely had time to leap backward instead.

For he heard a sharp, pinging sound, and he saw the great spar begin to move! The clevis had let go at last!

With a whispering, slithering noise the choker whipped loose from the anchoring stump. The end of the heavy cable of twisted steel swished within inches of Chuck's knees; if he hadn't backed up when he did, the thing would have caught him.

Too fast for the eye to follow, the choker slashed

around in a half-circle. Jarvis screamed, and Chuck saw the man's body jerked into the air, and flung a dozen feet away into the brush. With a whiplike crack the choker straightened out after coiling momentarily around Jarvis' legs; then, with an ominous thundering, the massive stick went hurtling down the slope.

Horrified, Chuck held his breath and watched it go, his lips involuntarily moving as he prayed. The stick seemed launched as true as the flight of an arrow in the direction of the cabin! Gramps and Kamooks were there!

A cloud of dust rolled up instantly behind the stick, and he could no longer see it. Breathlessly he waited, for what seemed to be hours. Then at last he heard a loud splash!

Almost dazed, he was suddenly aware that Tim stood beside him, and was saying, "Must have missed the cabin! Maybe the tip hit a stump or a big rock which turned it aside!" Tim's face was white, his eyes still wide with terror of the moment through which both of them had lived.

There was a groan from the brush where Jarvis had landed. "Help me!" he called. "My leg's busted!" Together they walked over to where the man lay.

His face was gray with pain. He lay on his back, one foot twisted aside at an odd angle. "Do somethin'!" he begged.

There was a light, padding sound behind them, and the boys turned. Kamooks, tongue lolling after his swift run up the hill, stood there expectantly, looking from Jarvis to the boys, as though asking what they wanted him to do. The very fact that the dog was here seemed to confirm what Tim had said, that the stick had missed the cabin. That meant Gramps was safe!

Tim told Jarvis, "We'll go back home and rig up some kind of stretcher so that we can carry you down the hill. Kamooks will stay with you until we get back. He won't bother you if you don't try any tricks!" To the wolf-dog he merely said, "Guard!" and pointed to Jarvis. Then he and Chuck went down the slope.

The quiet of a peaceful, summer afternoon in the San Juan Islands lay over Skookum-Chuck. Doc had completed his mission successfully. Bill Fuller's tug, carrying Sheriff Jim Dunham and two deputies, had come and gone, and on the return trip to the mainland, Lem Jarvis was aboard. Aside from a broken leg, he appeared to have no serious injuries. Chuck and Tim had bound rough splints to the leg as best they could, and the sheriff had said that the job would do until Jarvis reached the hospital, where he would be placed under guard until he recovered and was ready to stand trial as a log pirate. The stolen skiff, still in the cove, would be returned to its rightful owner on Shaw Island.

Gramps let out a gusty sigh of relief. "Lawsee!" he exclaimed. "Seems like I lived through a whole lifetime today. When that big stick come a-roarin' down the hill, I figured the world was about to come to its end. Pretty nigh happened, too, far as I'm concerned! But she hit somethin' and turned aside just in time."

Tim stirred restlessly, as though he didn't even want to think about the near-tragic outcome. He went out of the cabin, saying that he guessed it would be a good idea to buck up the runaway stick, get himself some more logs.

Chuck and Doc followed him. Outside, Tim turned to them, and said gloomily, "I suppose you fellows will be pulling out for Orcas Island now, so you can have your vacation after all. Well, we've had quite a time!" He tried to make it sound as indifferent as possible.

Yet Chuck understood. "Not unless you want it that way, Tim," he said reassuringly. "I think that Doc and I would like to stay here the rest of the summer. Not only are we having a real vacation, but we've already learned more about logging than we ever expected to. That can be important when we get to forestry school.

"In fact," he went on, "we'd like to help you cut enough logs so that you'll be able not only to finish high school, but to go on to college with us—forestry school. Why, you know the practical side of the logging game already!"

Tim choked. After a moment he said, "Thanks! I was hoping you'd say something like that." Then, as though embarrassed, he added "Well. let's buck up this stick!"

But Doc stopped him. There was a quizzical look in Doc's eyes. "I think," he said seriously, "that I owe you a sort of apology, Tim."

"Apology?"

"That first day at the cove," Doc explained, "I needled you pretty hard when you made fun of football. But what I was really trying to do was to make you so sore that you'd *want* to play, just to prove you could be good at it. Psychology stuff, see?"

Chuck groaned and muttered, "Oh, *brother!*"

Tim laughed outright. "You needn't apologize, Doc. The fact is, your needling had just the effect you wanted. I made up my mind I'd *show* you someday whether or not I could play football!"

Doc beamed with enthusiasm. "That's the talk!" he approved. "I've already decided that you'll be left halfback. And with the big horse, here," indicating Chuck, "running interference for you, the championship is as good as in the bag!"

"Hey!" Chuck broke in suddenly. "We're going to have visitors!"

From seaward came the steady thrumming of a powerful motor, and they saw a pontoon-equipped plane gliding low on the water toward them. Puzzled, they watched as the plane touched water, then taxied toward the float.

The pilot tossed Tim a line, which the boy made fast. Then the after-cabin door opened, and two men stepped out on the float. Chuck yelled, *"Dad!"* and sprang forward with outstretched arms toward the first passenger. The second seized Doc by the shoulders, shaking him gently.

Chuck stood back and eyed his father. The two looked much alike—the same features, the same sturdy build. "I thought," Chuck said, "that you and Mr. Peters were way up in Alaska!"

The elder Harmon smiled. "So we were," he replied. "But you forget that Seattle is only a few hours' flying time from Ketchikan. Your letter—well, it sounded mighty interesting. So we came home in a hurry. Arrived this morning. We hired this plane to fly us up here to the San Juans, just to see what you kids were doing!"

He faced Tim, held out his hand. "I can guess who *you* are!" he said with a smile. "Chuck told me in his letter. Meet Doc's father," he added, and the elder Peters likewise gave the Skookum-Chuck boy a warm handclasp.

Tim seemed flustered, yet he managed to say, "Please come up to the cabin. I want you to meet Gramps!"

"That," Harmon assured him, somewhat enigmatically, "is one of the reasons why both of us are here!" Tim looked up sharply, but said nothing.

The old man was seated as usual in his chair by the window as they walked in. He looked at them casually at first; then his eyes flew open. "Bull Harmon, so help me!" he breathed.

Chuck's father smilingly went over and took Gramps' hand. "Bull Harmon's son," he corrected.

He kept hold of Gramps' hand, and said, "And you, of course, are 'High Explosive' Elliott, about whom my father used to tell me all those thrilling stories when I was a youngster!"

Gramps flushed, yet his eyes twinkled happily. "Bull Harmon did that?" he asked. "Shucks, I can't believe it! Anyway, I reckon you didn't believe what he said. Bull always liked to make a good yarn out of hardly nothin' at all!"

"I doubt it!" Harmon's voice was firm. "He told me stories of the days when you and he were kings of the woods—and I believe them now just as I believed them then! He thought a lot of you, H.E.!"

Gramps sobered. "Reckon I always felt the same way about *him*," he confessed, "even though we had a ruckus over somethin' so triflin' that I've forgot what it was."

"I'm glad to hear that," Harmon replied. "That's the way it should be!" Then, as though to spare Gramps further confusion, he changed the subject. "What happened here, Chuck, since you wrote me?"

"Lemme tell the yarn!" Gramps begged eagerly.

When he had finished, Harmon nodded gravely, and turned to Peters. "Joe," he asked, "did you ever hear the like of it? I can't decide whether these kids of ours should be praised or punished! Still," and his eyes twinkled, "they've been having some real fun!"

"More fun than *we've* had lately!" Peters agreed with a smile.

"That's what I mean," Harmon went on. "I'm

hoping, Joe, that we can cut ourselves a piece of this cake!"

He faced Gramps again. "When Chuck wrote us about the old-growth timber on Skookum-Chuck Island," he went on, "it made Joe and me wonder if we haven't been overlooking something. So, we'd like to make a deal!"

"Deal?" There was doubt in Gramps' voice.

Harmon nodded. "Sound Logging Company," he explained, "is interested in the kind of timber you have here. Some of it must be big enough for veneer peeler blocks—and an eight-foot stick of *that* can be worth a hundred and fifty dollars! We'll pay you the standard stumpage rate for every tree we take. Also, we'll do the job in the latest scientific manner: Skyline rigs to carry logs over young timber so as not to destroy it, regular stands of old-growth trees left for reseeding purposes, and we'll even replant the cut-over area with seedling trees just to make sure that a new timber crop will be coming along. In that way, Skookum-Chuck Island can be kept green forever!

"It means," he concluded, "that you and your grandson won't have to worry about money for a long while, if ever. He can finish his education—forestry school, I suppose—and go on with his career. What do you think?"

Gramps did not answer at once. Finally he remarked rather shakily, "Almost too good to be true! But," and faint suspicion came into his voice, "you sure you ain't makin' this offer just because you want to do somethin' for me, on account Bull Harmon and

I used to be friends?" Pride showed in his eyes.

"I should say not!" Harmon told him emphatically. "We're interested in your timber. Trees of the size you have on this island are getting mighty scarce. This is strictly business!"

Gramps nodded, satisfied. "Then it's a deal!" he declared, and held out his hand.

Harmon took it. "One thing more," he said smilingly. "With this running start that Tim already has in this logging game, I can promise him a good job with our company when he's through at college. That will keep him with Chuck and Doc; seems to me it would be a shame to break up this combination!"

He put his hand on Gramps' shoulder. "I think, H.E.," he said gently, "that Bull Harmon would have liked it this way!"

Gramps nodded. Tears trickled down his wrinkled cheeks. Yet his face was bright with happiness.